ELAINE FORREST
VISITING NURSE

Books by Lois Hobart

KATIE AND HER CAMERA
A PALETTE FOR INGRID
LAURIE, PHYSICAL THERAPIST
STRANGERS AMONG US
ELAINE FORREST, VISITING NURSE

ELAINE FORREST
VISITING NURSE

2212

BY LOIS HOBART

Discard

JULIAN MESSNER, INC. • NEW YORK

Published by Julian Messner, Inc.
8 West 40 Street, New York 18

Published simultaneously in Canada
by The Copp Clark Publishing Co. Limited

The Library of Congress has cataloged this publication as follows:

Hobart, Lois.
  Elaine Forrest, visiting nurse. New York, Messner [1959]
  192 p.   21 cm.
  A novel.

———————

  I. Title.

PZ7.H64El   813.5   59–7134‡

Printed in the United States of America

ACKNOWLEDGMENT

Writing a vocational novel requires the help of many different people and associations, and I should like here to pay my respects to them, named or unnamed.

In particular I wish to thank:

Dr. Brumfield, Public Health Commissioner, Westchester County, White Plains, N. Y.

Miss Dorothy Clark, Public Health Department, Westchester County, White Plains, N. Y.

Dr. Theodore Drachman, Public Health Commissioner, Columbia County, N. Y.

Mrs. Sylvia Bellos, District Nursing Association, Director, Mt. Kisco, N. Y., and her whole staff, who have been so cooperative.

Mrs. Eleanor Hendrickson, Katonah Public Library, Katonah, N. Y.

Mrs. Roland Berg, former public health nurse.

I should like to add my thanks to the nurses who were kind enough to let me observe their visits and office duties and to their patients, who gave me further insight into the problems and rewards of public health nursing. If this book helps to bring into the field more of the much-needed nurses of high caliber, it will be a great satisfaction.

Lois Hobart

CHAPTER ONE

First days were important—Elaine Forrest could remember the very tone of her father's voice the first time he had said that. It was the day, following the lonely summer of her mother's death, that he had brought her to the boarding school on Chicago's Michigan Boulevard.

It was his attempt to cheer her up and enliven her first departure from home; and in the same precise lawyer's way that he had once explained chess moves to her in early childhood, he had explained that first days set a tone and offered clues to the experiences that would follow. It was like a chess game to watch, ponder, evaluate, and come up with a surmise.

It wasn't the kind of game that would work with most children, but Elaine had risen to his challenge and quite often found that her first surmise gave intimations of the actual experience that followed. It was a game that she carried past school days into college, into nurse's training, into her first job as a hospital nurse. So now she rested her head against the window of the train and watched its lurching, creaking progress along the countryside toward Kahopac and wondered what this day would bring.

She was usually right in her evaluations of people too. Certainly about Bryce Thorne the day she had first glimpsed him when he came to his sister's birthday party just long enough to present her with a new tennis racket and meet her friends. Even then, without knowing him, Elaine had made up her mind that this was the kind of man she would like to marry when she grew up. Even then the outlines of the kind of life she wanted to shape for herself were quite clear to her, and Bryce fitted into it. He had been so gracious to his sister's guests, not at all like a condescending college student. She remembered him with absolute clarity—the face that was just a little too round and smooth and boyish to be handsome, the blond hair neatly brushed with a wave at the temples, the manner so gently courteous, so nice and unspoiled by wealth and position.

Years later when she was in college and of an age suitable for a young physics researcher, her first date with him confirmed her liking for him. He even met her father's rigorous standards, and that probing legal mind could find no objections to their engagement.

"Kahopac next, next stop Kahopac." The conductor went through the car plucking out the tickets from the seat rims, and passed her. The familiar name failed to register and Elaine went on dreaming.

"Excuse me, but isn't Kahopac your stop?" The young man across the aisle rested a duffel bag on the arm of his seat and waited with a little grin for her startled jump. "No hurry—a couple of minutes yet. Want some help with that bag?" He reached up and brought down the handsome blue and gray suitcase for her. "Heavy. Bricks in it?"

"Thank you." Her voice struck the exact note of proper thanks for his reminder, no more, no less, and for his courtesy in helping with the bag; but her reserve and polite smile discouraged any further conversation beyond her reply of, "No, a few books." She was well accustomed to gauging the proper degree of cordiality or coolness with young men and had found her accuracy an excellent defense against the brash and undesired attentions of casual acquaintances.

8

Since there was time, Elaine opened her pocketbook, fished out an enamel compact, and touched her brown bangs to ensure the slightly irregular line she liked under her velveteen beret. Her face had delicacy with character; it was more than a pretty face. The thick, unplucked brows framed fine blue-gray eyes, the nose was straight and a trifle long above the rather wide mouth. When she clicked her compact shut and dropped it back into her purse, the young man was still standing there like an amused satyr.

The train creaked to a halt, and he reached for her suitcase before she could take it. Inwardly she shrugged and noted that this young man required a little more discouragement than most, or else he was more obtuse. No, he didn't look obtuse. His eyes were too quick and alert, too amused, too penetrating a blue. He had already sized up her trim, exceedingly well-tailored blue-gray suit and her assurance.

The conductor helped her down the steps and smiled good-by at her and swung back on.

"Is someone coming to meet you? Or could you use a lift?" the young man said in his friendly, casual way.

"Someone is meeting me, thank you." She surveyed the station for signs of Doc—Dr. Todd O'Brien. She withdrew a step when he set her bag down, as if to underscore her refusal.

"It's only that there are few cabs here," he explained, "and I didn't want you to be stranded."

"It's good of you to be concerned," Elaine said with the merest hint of sarcasm in her soft, well-bred voice, "but I daresay I can cope with the situation." Just as she had expected, the fellow could be a nuisance with his persistence.

"Yes, I daresay you could cope with most situations," he said with a dry mockery that marked her dismissal and tossed it into the September breeze. "Well, as long as you're taken care of, good-by." Whistling, he turned on his heels, walked off with a swing of his duffel bag, crossed the parking lot, and moved among the cars to a drab, paint-worn, scarred little Plymouth that stood inches above the late models around it.

He was certainly not a type that appealed to her. Too casual, with a tieless open-collared shirt and the tweed jacket slung over his shoulder. There was something too—not irresponsible exactly, not fresh, not precisely unreliable but—uncertain, *unpredictable*, that was it. And Elaine liked *predictables*: actions, situations, people that she could interpret and antici- pate and deal with. Even that crest of light brown hair of his was too wild, too erratic with a life of its own.

Her momentary fretfulness faded. No need to bother about him any more, but where was Doc? Probably an emergency of some sort, but she was disappointed; he had promised to be there with bells on to take her to the hotel and to meet her new boss at Visiting Nurse Association headquarters.

It was a pity. Elaine had counted on him to be her link between her old familiar life and this new one, but if he didn't come in another fifteen minutes she had better call a cab. Or maybe Connie O'Brien would pick her up if Doc were delayed. Elaine had just started for the waiting room of the station when a little Volkswagen squealed to a stop and Doc unfolded him- self from the driver's seat.

"Elaine, Elaine, how are you? How's your father? You're looking as stunning as ever, girl—you'll overwhelm this town, I'm afraid. Come, squeeze into my little jalopy and we'll be off."

Elaine laughed outright. The cereal-advertisement poster on the station behind him was so apt a description of Doc. " 'Snap, Crackle, Pop', still just like the cereals, aren't you? It's good to see you, and Dad's missed you terribly."

Doc's very beard bristled on his chin; the thick eyebrows moved with their own vitality on the sharp-featured face, and he was electric with energy.

"How is Connie? I can't imagine her living in the country, she's so urbane."

"Oh, we love it here, Elaine. You never took a wiser step in your life than in applying for this job in public health. Good for you to get away from the city, time to cut those home ties anyhow, my girl. If your father had any sense he'd cut loose those legal cords that are throttling him and retire to a place like this. Much better for his health—and he should watch himself. How does he get along without me to look after him?"

"He's fine. Chicago's his idea of Paradise, and you know he won't retire; he's too wrapped up in his work."

"Well, he can't say I haven't warned him times enough. One of these days he'll end up in the hospital with a heart attack, not just a lung risection." Doc puffed indignantly. "Stubborn man, your father." He shot Elaine a wicked look. "And you're cut out of the same cloth, my girl. Reminds me, trunk coming later, if I know you."

Elaine dimpled. "Yes, Dad will send it on when he knows my permanent address. I can't be in uniform all the time."

"Probably not much of the time. In some offices there's a set policy about dressing in uniform, but here we let the girls decide. The older nurses generally like to wear uniforms, and feel they give a sort of status or authority. Younger nurses usually prefer street clothes, and some patients prefer it—would rather not have it obvious that a nurse visits them. Most likely you'll wear uniforms mainly for maternity clinics and such."

He shifted gears, looking a little uncomfortable as he continued to speak. "There's something I want to get off my mind, Elaine. Connie's giving me a guilt complex, says I talked you into trying this job and she's worried that you might not like it here. She thinks you're too much of a city girl. In a way she's right—on the surface of it, it doesn't look like the spot for you. But you know me and my hunches. I'm convinced that you'll end up loving it here; but it's only fair to warn you again that the first few weeks or months are likely to be tough for you, coming as you do from such a different background."

"Oh, Doc, don't give it another thought. You can't scare me off. You gave me a good sales talk but I made up my own mind, thank you; and if I made the wrong choice—which I don't for a moment believe—that's my bad luck and I'll have to figure out what to do about it. I'll manage."

He grinned back at her, relieved. "Always ready to tackle anything, that's my girl." He nodded at a little white cottage they were passing. "That's where Kitty Gullen lives with a couple of stewardesses. She's one of your colleagues."

"What about the others?"

"Some of them grew up around here and live with their families. Some got married and have homes of their own. Sometimes they share an apartment or a house or room somewhere. We're shorthanded now, by the way. Mrs. Hagstrom lives across the Connecticut border with her own family and commutes."

"She sounded so nice in her letters."

"Fine woman, wonderful nursing background. Private nursing, hospital supervisor, army service in Japan, industrial nursing, school nurse—she's been in almost every phase of nursing. Had to: her husband's an engineer and they've lived all over. But when her husband retired, she came back to her first love; public health. She does a splendid job as head of our Visiting Nurse Association. We're lucky to get her." He gave Elaine another of his quick looks. "I hope you realize your luck in landing this job here. It's one of the oldest and best rural public health staffs in the country and we usually have a waiting list of nurses, but we had a rash of marriages this summer and three of the girls had to leave town because their husbands were transferred or drafted or something. And mind you,

12

I didn't use any pull to get you the job; it was all on your record. All I did was tell you about the chance."

"Much appreciated, Doc."

The town looked minuscule to Elaine after the broad avenues of Chicago and the expanse of stores, skyscrapers, parks, and apartment buildings. It was hardly larger than the town near the Forrest summer cottage in Michigan, although she had to admit that these shops were cleaner and more modern and would have looked at home on a side street in Chicago or New York. The courthouse and many buildings were in the Colonial tradition, but there was a high school and a parochial school of contemporary design.

Kahopac was an attractive place, she decided, wondering if the town had changed much since her mother lived here as a young girl. It was set among sloping hills and rocky cliffs with a generous array of tall, century-old trees lining the streets. The houses were mostly well-kept, freshly painted Colonial homes with nice lawns, with a sprinkling of modern homes of redwood or stone or brick.

The Volkswagen came to a stop in front of a spreading white frame building with a long veranda. It was unpretentious, old, mellow with welcome, spruce with fresh white paint and black shuttered windows.

"Here's the hotel. You can register, get rid of your bag, and then we'll get over to the office."

In ten minutes Elaine was back and they drove along the business section up a hill to the large brick house that served as headquarters for the V.N.A. They passed through the back door into a corridor, past a glassed-off section that housed a cheerful middle-aged telephone operator-receptionist who waved them in with a smile to the small office in the front.

Mrs. Hagstrom had just dropped the telephone into its cradle and rose to welcome them.

Elaine held out her hand with a smile. "I'm so happy to meet you, Mrs. Hagstrom."

"You come with very high recommendations, Miss Forrest," said Mrs. Hagstrom in a pleasant, soft voice. But the kind, keen eyes retained a certain distance, a guarded appraisal, and Elaine understood that this woman was to be won over not by agreeable manners but by solid performance. She promised herself that before too long there would be the wholehearted approval she had been used to. "We're happy to have you with us. Since we're not very formal around here, you won't mind if I call you Elaine, will you?"

"Please do. Good-by, Dr. O'Brien. Thank you for bringing me over."

Mrs. Hagstrom glanced at her watch. "We have time for a look around the office, and then I thought it would be a good idea to take you with me on some calls this afternoon. Since we're so shorthanded I've been taking over some of your predecessor's duties."

Across the corridor was a large conference room with a marble fireplace, a long table, and several folding chairs and a few armchairs. Upstairs was a kitchen that the nurses used for preparing lunches and the volunteer aides used for preparing packs and sterilizing equipment for the nurses' bags. Next to it was another large room with several desks, a couple of typewriters on portable tables, file cabinets, a water fountain, and some spare chairs set about a long table in the center of the room.

Mrs. Hagstrom showed Elaine a cubicle at the side just large enough for a desk, two chairs, a typewriter, and bookcases.

"This is where Frieda Manship talks with the nurses or clients about cases. She's our social-worker consultant and is here usually three mornings a week, oftener if necessary. We use this room as a library when she's not here or occasionally for a private discussion with a doctor about a patient."

She indicated a desk near a window. "This will be your desk. In the top drawer you'll find brochures and pamphlets of information about our services and policies, a list of agencies and telephone numbers you'll need, and so on. Tomorrow Kitty Gullen or Molly Carew will show you the essentials to carry in your black bag. The bathroom is over there near Frieda's office. Now I believe we have time to stop at the hospital."

The hospital was a conventional brick building, sizable for the community but small compared to the large institutions Elaine had studied and worked in in Chicago. It was well kept, from the smooth lawn and hedges outside to the spotless interior.

"Strange how quickly you sense the atmosphere of a place," Elaine remarked as they walked down the corridor. "Something about the way the nurses and attendants move about their business. They're quick and purposeful and yet have time for a smile."

It was one of the things she had disliked at the Chicago hospital she had worked in—the coldness, the insistence upon protocol, the rigid distinctions between doctors, head nurses, supervisors, student nurses, aides, practical nurses, orderlies, and the new young R.N.'s. To Elaine, accustomed to attention as an outstanding student, a personality, and a social asset, it had been irritating to encounter such stratification and formalities. It was pleasant to find that hospitals existed where respect and liking were accorded to you as an individual and not on the basis of your function or status.

Mrs. Hagstrom gave her an approving glance. "This is a very well-administered hospital, and the county supports it well. This wing is the physical-therapy division." She halted at a door and waved at a husky young man who was lifting a child into a butterfly tank to exercise a withered leg. "That's Philip Roland, the physical therapist on our staff; you'll meet him tomorrow. You will find him very helpful with many of your patients, and he's clever about inventing gadgets for manipulating invalids. On the other side of the coffee shop and lounge is the new wing for laboratory, X-ray division, and some much-needed new wards. Oh, here's another colleague. Miss Schwartz, I'd like you to meet our newest nurse, Elaine Forrest."

One look at Miss Schwartz explained why first names were not used in her case, if indeed so monumental a person even possessed anything so trivial. She was a large older woman dressed in a dark blue uniform and hat, with iron-gray hair in a short, no-nonsense cut, who moved with a long, stately pace that made Elaine wonder whether she marched to an inward dirge or followed some funereal trail. Behind rimless glasses her face was square and impassive. Her smile was stiff and remote. She greeted them briefly in a sepulchral voice and continued down the hall toward the entrance.

Following more leisurely, Elaine and Mrs. Hagstrom went on talking. "From the entrance you can see the building where we hold our maternity clinics, over there. Oh, there's Kitty Gullen coming from it now."

At the door of the clinic a girl appeared—not a girl so much as a sprite who danced rather than walked down the steps and along the path to the hospital. She hallooed at Miss Schwartz, who halted like a battleship coming to rest at sea. Elaine watched the two together, one looming tall, dark, and forbidding, the other tiny and dynamic, restlessly mobile even during the short chat. The girl whirled with a laugh and came running up the steps of the hospital.

"Ah, this must be Elaine Forrest," said Kitty Gullen, holding out a small hand before Mrs. Hagstrom could perform an introduction. Not a brogue but a lilt was there in the warm voice. "I'm delighted to meet you. One more pair of hands to relieve the burdens." Closer, Elaine caught the twinkle in the green eyes—naturally with that coppery hair and translucent skin they would be green. Clearly no official status could erase the laugh lines and gaiety of those eyes or long impose the shackles of dignity. Elaine couldn't help succumbing.

"Where will you be staying? Would you like to move in with me until you find a place? One of my roommates is off on a month's vacation so we have lots of room."

"That's awfully nice of you, but I've already registered in the hotel and this should be a good time to find an apartment, I think. May I take a rain check if I get stuck?"

Momentarily Elaine toyed with the idea of sharing Kitty's place, but dismissed it. She really would prefer a place where she could be alone, do what she chose, keep what hours she liked, and not find someone hanging stockings in the bathroom at all hours or popping in to borrow a jacket or chat when she wanted to rest or do chores. No, it would be better to find a place of her own with some privacy.

"I'm afraid I'll have to run along now; I'm late again, Mrs. H., after I swore to keep my appointments on the dot this week. Isn't that awful? I mustn't keep Dr. Kennedy waiting. Elaine, I'll see you in the office tomorrow. We usually gather there to do a few chores before we go off for our calls. Maybe we can have lunch together. Bye."

CHAPTER TWO

"We still have a little time to talk," Mrs. Hagstrom said as they returned to her car, "and I've been wondering what made you take up nursing. We don't get many girls from wealthy families, especially in public health, where we make calls at every kind of home, from the wealthy to the poorest shacks and tenements."

Elaine's habit of reserve yielded to the sense that her usual pat response—a conventional "It's important work and I wanted to be of service instead of being a social butterfly" speech— would be inacceptable to Mrs. Hagstrom. She found herself wanting to answer as honestly as she knew how.

Her ordinarily softly assured tone of voice altered subtly into something more uncertain and questing. "Well—I suppose it started with my mother's illness a dozen years ago. I suppose the nurses made a pet of me because I was around the hospital so much. They took me into the laboratory for reports and X rays, into the kitchen when they picked up Mother's meals, into the nurses' room, even into the operating theater when it wasn't in use. They seemed to know so much and it was all very mysterious and hushed and wonderful."

The images surged back powerfully: the kind-faced special nurse, the student nurses pretty and starched in their crisp uniforms and pinafores and caps, the head nurse with the authority and mien of a stern Athena, the young interns who joked with the little girl with Alice in Wonderland hair who was so prim, contained, serious, and ever-curious. And the strong, clean smells, the soft rubber-soled footfalls of nurses passing through the halls, the lights dimmed at night, the whole hospital aura. And then piercingly again that terrible day when she ran into her mother's room and a stranger looked back at her with glazed, unknowing eyes, eyes that pushed her daughter far away. After that day it seemed that her mother had vanished, long before the actual death.

But in the shorthand of communication with a new acquaintance, even so kind a one as Mrs. Hagstrom, this could not be voiced. Eliptically Elaine went on: "When my mother died, it stopped being a pageant, and I tried to push it all out of my mind. Then, years later, my father went into the same hospital —I can still remember getting the shakes when I went there with him—I knew he had to have a lung risection and I was terrified that he would die. Thank goodness Dr. O'Brien stayed with me the whole time Dad was on the operating table, until we were fairly sure the operation was successful.

"I think that was the turning point for me. By then I was old enough to understand how vital nursing care was, how much more it involved than taking temperatures, changing the patient's position, showing charts to the doctor. It struck me that if a nurse would put up with so many unpleasant things, like helping patients use bedpans, changing bandages, giving hypos, and all that, she must find her work very absorbing. When Dad was discharged, the nurse came to the door with us, and something in her face—not simply pleasure that he was able to go home with me but the knowledge that part of his recovery had lain in her hands and she had done her work well —something made me wonder what it was like to hold a life in your hands, to battle death and disease. After that I couldn't get it out of my mind."

She gave a little laugh. "My father wasn't so keen on the idea, but Bryce—my fiancé—encouraged me, and of course Dr. O'Brien was delighted. I suppose that somewhere underneath was the feeling that by becoming a nurse I was in a sense helping to pay for my father's life—does that sound silly? So I went through college and nursing school and had six months at the hospital and then I applied for this job." She gave Mrs. Hagstrom an uncharacteristically shy look and half apologized for the intimacy of her story. "I'm sorry. I didn't mean to——"

"Oh, goodness, there's nothing to apologize for. But what made you think of public health? And why here? That's Dr. O'Brien's work, no doubt."

"In a way, yes. Probably I wouldn't have thought of public health except that when he moved here to practice and became part-time public health officer he used to write so enthusiastically about his work and the nursing staff here. But what clinched it was that my mother——"

"Here we are at the Tollivers'. When we finish here, Elaine, I'd like to hear more." The car had drawn up in front of a fresh, neat ranchhouse in a tidy new development.

The visit was merely to give a cortisone injection to an elderly patient, but the length of their stay seemed all out of proportion to the purpose of the visit. Afterward Elaine inquired with unconscious oblique criticism, "Does each visit require so long a time?"

Mrs. Hagstrom was scribbling notes in her memo book. "Three dollars, that brings them up to date; they pay regularly, every other visit." Meditatively she tapped a pencil against her lips. "I must check with their doctor and see if he doesn't agree that Mr. Tolliver might begin to do a little work now around home. . . . Did it seem a long visit? I was so busy considering what he might be ready for and observing his reactions that the time slipped by. But it's usually time well spent. We try to make each visit count educationally too, making housewives aware of safety practices, health hazards, and so on. I see they put up a gate by that short flight of stairs so their granddaughter won't fall when she visits them. They often take care of her."

The next stop was a visit with a child who had cerebral palsy. The youngster looked reticent and glum, but two older children ran in and out of the house like little Indians throughout the discussion as to the wisdom of sending the little boy to a school for cerebral-palsy children.

In the car Mrs. Hagstrom again made notes, frowning a little. "Frieda was right in predicting that the father would be against it. He has some kind of guilt feelings about the child's ailment —you'll find this quite often—and wants to keep the child home. The mother is devoted to Billy but is more sensible about it; she feels that he would improve and learn to do more for himself if he were under expert care. She doesn't think that it's fair to spend so much time with him when the other children need her attention and love too. It would be a struggle for them financially, but she thinks that they could manage and that there would be less stress in the home. . . . Well, Mrs. Flandrau next. Only a Vitamin B injection there."

A mile south on the highway they turned up a narrow asphalt road that serpentined past four or five houses to the crest of a pine-covered hill. "Mrs. Flandrau's sister left recently to be with her sick daughter, and I think Mrs. Flandreau has found it pretty lonely, although her maid lives with her. She's been a widow about fifteen years now."

They drove through the entrance of a high stone wall into a courtyard and found themselves facing a villa-like house dating from perhaps the 1920's. Dark stucco, almost quaint, supplemented by stonework to provide a solid framework. It was rather a large house and gave a marvelous sense of privacy and security; possibly because of the courtyard screened by the high wall and towering pine trees.

A middle-aged Negress came to the door and with pleasant, soft greetings admitted them to the foyer. In front of them a wide staircase rose to a small landing and then turned left to the second floor. From the top of the staircase a disembodied voice floated down: "Tell them I'll be down directly, Cora. I'm just brushing my hair."

Cora ushered them into the living room, a large, dim room surprisingly furnished with a variety of Oriental and Occidental chairs, tables and *objets d'art*. An enormous Persian rug covered almost the whole floor.

"What a weird mixture," Elaine murmured.

"Yes, strange, isn't it?" Mrs. Hagstrom said. "Her husband represented a New York bank and lived all over the East and in South America too. He died not very long after they built this house."

"She must lead a pretty lonely life."

"More so now than a few years ago. Friends still visit her at times from all over the world and her sister spends a good deal of time with her, and Cora takes wonderful care of her. She's a very active woman for her years."

"Oh?" It didn't sound like a very appealing kind of life to Elaine. Admiringly she touched a handsome Chinese horse on the mantel and her sleeve knocked over a small gold picture frame nearby. She set it back in place, noting the faintly hawkish dark good looks of the young man in the frame. He looked foreign—Indian? South American? Not Mrs. Flandrau's son, surely, since Mrs. Hagstrom had mentioned no children.

"Will you have some tea with me?" came a gentle voice, this time from the doorway arch. Mrs. Flandrau might almost have been reconstructed from the sound of her voice. There was gentility with gentleness, there were fine features a little

22

blurred with the lines and wrinkles of the years, snowy, soft hair, the still-erect ladylike carriage and deportment, and fine eyes barely faded from their youthful blue. Perhaps in her seventies, Elaine judged as she held out her hand.

"Your new nurse?" Mrs. Flandrau added with a disarming smile to Mrs. Hagstrom. The hand Elaine clasped was small and fine too, but firm. "We have a few good things if you're interested in Oriental or Hispano-American art. After Mrs. Hagstrom gives me my vitamins I'll be happy to show you around. If she will permit me, I'll first take you out to the terrace."

"Thank you, I'd like that," Elaine said politely, and followed the old lady out through the French windows. "Oh, what a wonderful sight," she exclaimed, really struck by the view. Hidden by the house and stone wall in their approach, the vista she saw came as a brilliant surprise, as if a jeweler had opened an unimpressive little box and displayed an exquisite brooch of pearls and rubies. "I had no idea you were so high here."

The terrace looked down upon two lakes bordered by highways and firs and willows, beautifully pocketed in the valley between the mountains. At least to Elaine's prairie-bred eyes, used to the plains of Illinois and the low woodlands of the shores of Lake Michigan, the hills looked like mountains. A few yellowing leaves sifted down in the breeze and in the sinking sun there was a trace of russet over the wooded hills. A few orange rays lit up the second floor of the stuccoed house above them and picked out a little iron-railed balcony.

When Mrs. Hagstrom had given the injection, their hostess conducted Elaine through the rest of the house, clearly pleased at her interest in the eclectic furnishings of the house, from the heavy mission style of the dining room to the last Colonial bedroom upstairs.

This room quite charmed Elaine. The bed was canopied and spread with a dazzling white quilted cloth and mounded with pillows. On the floor lay two hooked oval rugs. There were a couple of caned chairs, a beautiful, lustrous old rocking chair, and an armchair with a cane footstool. In a corner near a window stood a lovely, simple old desk. An oval Colonial mirror surmounted a high chest of drawers.

How different it was from Elaine's tailored room in her apartment at home, with its corduroy-clad couch-bed and corduroy hangings keyed in a dark blue to the pale blue of the carpet and pillows and upholstered chair, with its very modern Herman Miller chests, desk, and tables, with its walk-in closets and its handsomely appointed bathroom. The restraint of sleek modern in contrast to the restraint of mellow Colonial simplicity.

From the crisp-curtained window that opened onto the little balcony she had seen from the terrace, Elaine glimpsed another house through the trees half a mile away.

"What a charming, charming room!" And quite to her own surprise, on impulse she turned to Mrs. Flandrau. "How I'd love to live in this room! Is there any chance——?"

She stopped abruptly, intimidated by her own half-suggestion and embarrassed at the very notion of distressing this gentle old lady, who obviously never needed to concern herself with any thought of money, with the remotest allusion to the commercial, even if she chanced to look kindly on the absurd idea of allowing a stranger to share her home.

The old lady lifted an eyebrow at Elaine. "Do I understand you to mean that you would like to live here?" she inquired delicately. She mused for a moment and Elaine had a distinct feeling of undergoing an appraisal.

"It might be a very good idea," Mrs. Flandrau murmured. "It would be company . . . It would be nice to know that in

an emergency a nurse was handy . . . if anything should happen
. . . Cora would be less worried . . . Yes," she assented with
abrupt decisiveness, and went on to deal with the mundane
aspects of her decision. "Let me think—what would be cus-
tomary, I wonder? You would want breakfast in the morning,
yes? Ah, how nice to share a breakfast again, indeed yes, and
Cora will be happy to have a heartier appetite and fresh palate
to serve. Oh, dear, I hope that slender figure of yours is deceiv-
ing or Cora will be disappointed. An excellent cook, Cora, and
it distresses her that my appetite no longer offers a stimulus to
her culinary skill. Yes, Cora will be pleased, and she is strong
and will not mind a little extra work. She, too, would like company, I believe. Yes, yes, yes. Would you care to take dinners
with us too? No, no, perhaps your hours are irregular or you
might not wish to return if you have a—a date, as they say. No,
not dinners," Mrs. Flandrau continued reflectively. "Now as to
financial arrangements—let me think. Would fifteen dollars a
week be fair? Satisfactory to you? Are we agreed? Good. That
is settled."

Inwardly Elaine gasped. How quickly and efficiently her implication had been seized, accepted, dealt with, and dismissed
with no trace of embarrassment. And certainly no evidence of a
cloudy mind, whatever her age.

With the matter now settled, Elaine began to be fretted with
un-Forrest-like doubts and qualms. Like her father, she was
accustomed to evaluating, making decisions, and proceeding
without casting a backward glance. But this was different. She
somehow felt that there was some sort of emotional involve-
ment, which made her uneasy.

She might have been better off with the privacy and independence of a hotel or in her own apartment, or even sharing
one with another nurse. This might prove an odd and lonely
sort of household. Elaine couldn't guess whether Mrs. Flandrau

might treat her as a sort of crutch for her loneliness—although that seemed unlikely, for Mrs. Flandrau scarcely appeared to be a clinging vine—or as a protégé, which Elaine would not like either. It puzzled her that she could not find a proper category for Mrs. Flandrau. The gentle breeding resided oddly with the practicality and efficiency that had flashed out so candidly.

Why had she been so impulsive, so unlike herself as not to consider the consequences before she spoke?

Turning for a final half-rueful appraisal of the room, Elaine caught a glimpse of herself in the oval mirror. Her gray eyes were clouded and, chameleonlike, had shaded into a blue that reflected the color of her high-collared suit; the brown hair had become a little tumbled in the wind on the terrace, and it seemed that the girl in the mirror had taken on some of the mellow russet glow of the room itself. Mirror, mirror on the wall, is this the place for me?

CHAPTER THREE

Now that the photographs of her father and mother were on the mantel of the fireplace, Elaine felt the room was truly hers. The Olympia portable typewriter stood enclosed in its case by the desk. The bookshelf was filled with a few dozen cherished books—novels, reference works, paper-back books. *Alice in Wonderland* and Eleanor Farjeon's *Martin Pippin* cheek by jowl with Dostoevski's *Idiot*, Cozzen's *Guard of Honor*, Mann's *Buddenbrooks* and *Magic Mountain*, T. H. White's *The Sword in the Stone* and Kipling's *Rewards and Fairies* consorting amiably with John Masters' *Far, Far the Mountain Peak*, and Joyce Cary's *Mister Johnson*.

Cora, bringing in a terra-cotta vase of roses for the mantel, stopped to admire the photographs. "Your mother, Miss Forrest? What a beautiful lady? You look alike, don't you?"

It was the last photograph taken of her mother, a few months before she entered the hospital. Elaine pushed back her hair. "Not really. Her coloring was different, very blonde, with brown eyes, and her features were more delicate. But I suppose there's a resemblance."

"Yes, I think that's why she has a familiar look." Cora picked up the other photograph. "Your father reminds me a little of . . . no, I guess not. If it weren't for the mustache . . . He looks very distinguished."

That was what everyone said about her father. Distinguished

and awesomely stern. But Elaine knew how to melt the stern-ness. She smiled and placed the third photograph on her desk —Bryce in cap and gown when he received his Ph.D. Her favorite because he looked so grave and important, though Bryce disliked it, saying it looked too pompous and solemn.

"Oh, Miss Forrest, isn't he handsome! Your young man?"

"My young man," Elaine smiled. "Speaking of young men, Cora, who is the man in the picture on the mantel downstairs?"

"Ah, Señor Carlos, Miss Forrest. It is many years since we've seen him. He's the son of friends of Mrs. Flandrau in South America. When I first came to work for Mrs. Flandrau he used to visit here. He was a student then. Such a nice young man, so full of jokes and fun."

It was obvious that Cora was happy with the prospect of more company and Elaine decided to forestall further inti-macies and exchanges, which might become intrusive. "Ah, well, I guess I must settle down to work," she said pleasantly. She picked up a stack of brochures and leaflets that Mrs. Hag-strom had given her to look over. "Cora, would you wake me about seven-thirty tomorrow? That should give me plenty of time to be in the office by eight-thirty."

Promptly at eight-thirty she reported to Mrs. Hagstrom in her small office. Already busy at the telephone, Mrs. Hagstrom gave Elaine a smile and a shrug of helplessness while she con-tinued speaking. In a moment she covered the phone with her hand to say, "Elaine, Philip Roland is upstairs at his desk. You remember, the physical therapist you saw at the hospital. He'll introduce you to everyone and show you your desk. I'm stuck with this call, but you run along."

Obediently Elaine went upstairs. Philip Roland was tilted back in his chair studying a record. When she entered, he let his chair down with a crash.

"You're Elaine, aren't you? There's your desk right by the door in front of Kitty's. Stash your things away there and you can hang up your coat in that closet. Oops, excuse me." The phone began to ring and he answered it.

As Elaine set her purse on the desk, she noted another stack of pamphlets and books ready for her perusal. Not much protocol here, that was plain. Very different from the hospital starch that stiffened everything from the uniform to manners. Elaine hadn't cared for the hospital hierarchy and regimen, but she wasn't sure she liked this much informality either. Still, if that's the way it was, she had better get used to it.

The others seemed to come in in waves, first Miss Schwartz and Molly Carew, who gave Elaine an irresistibly friendly smile and set her black bag on a desk acros the room while she cheerfully complained, "Oh, those stairs—*when* do we rate an escalator for these old bones? So, our new Nightingale, Elaine Forrest, right?"

Elaine had to laugh. "I'm beginning to feel like a celebrity with everyone knowing me."

"It's the office grapevine," said Molly, lowering herself with a sigh into her chair.

Phil hung up the phone and grinned at her. "Our Gibraltar, Elaine. Ask her any question about this area and she can tell you the answer, from the population to who founded the town and whose dog is having pups."

"Phil, stop making me out to be Methuselah just because I've been around here forever and six days. I'm not a day over fifty-four." There was an easy amplitude to Molly's short figure but no suggestion of flabbiness under the blue uniform; her movements were quick and her blue eyes twinkling and alert. "Frieda coming in today for consultation? I have a good Social Work Problem for her to cut her teeth on."

From the doorway Mrs. Hagstrom laughed. "Now be fair,

Molly. She's been very useful to the other girls. You don't expect her to acquire your experience with people in a couple of years of work, do you? She can't help it that you were born knowing all about people."

"Hoot, listen to the woman. Stop buttering me up or I'll think you want me to make another speech to the P.T.A."

"Molly, would you show Elaine how we pack our bags and what we carry. I have to meet with the Board this morning, so if you'd take over . . . Good."

A tall, thin girl came through the doorway as Mrs. Hagstrom left, and Molly introduced her as Frieda Manship. The girl said hello and went on to her little cubicle, while Molly unloaded her bag on Elaine's desk to show her the contents—red book of records for keeping track of payments, nominal in most cases, pencils, syringes autoclaved for clinic use, small porcelain tray, hand towels, alcohol bottle, forceps, beige money bag for fees collected, green liquid soap, Lysol, Merthiolate for antiseptic, cotton balls, Vaseline, thermometers sterilized in alcohol, apron, adhesives, bandages, scissors, and heaven knew what else. Elaine watched, hynotized by the flying fingers and amazed that such a variety of objects could be so compactly packed.

Molly was showing her how to make out records and daily assignment sheets when Kitty Gullen came running up the stairs.

"Heard the news?" she cried, dumping her bag on the paper-littered desk behind Elaine's.

"What's up, courier?" Phil inquired from across the room.

"New consultant," Kitty announced in a stage whisper with a glance at the door to Frieda's cubicle.

"Not another," groaned Molly. "We're just learning to cope with Frieda and her ideas and terminology."

"Well, not really," Kitty confessed. "This one's some kind of observer. Something to do with family diagnosis."

"And that's a fancy name for what?" Molly asked.

Kitty shrugged and sat down. "Getting the whole picture of family relationships that affect the patient is my guess. Same thing the general practitioner has been doing for years, probably."

"Who's the consultant or observer or whatever?" Phil wanted to know.

"Dirk Yaeger. He'll tell us about it at the next conference. Ever hear of him, Molly? He lived around here once."

"Dirk Yaeger?" Molly mused for a moment. "Might be Annie Dunne's nephew. He lived here for a few years after his father died. Nice boy, as I recall. Hope he didn't latch on to Annie's eccentricities."

"She still living alone on that broken-down farm?" Phil asked.

"Yes, and that reminds me, Phil; I'd like you to stop in with me this week and give her some exercises for her bad arm. She's been having trouble since she broke it last spring, and gave me a call yesterday."

"Well, if no one's interested in my news . . ." Kitty pouted in an extravagant parody of offended dignity and brushed her fingernails briskly against her gray dress."

"Ho! Try and stop you," snorted Molly. "All right, what's the rest of the story?"

"To be perfect honest, I don't know much about it, but I ran into Dr. O'Brien and he told me. Yaeger's a graduate student, a sociologist who's making a study for his Ph.D., and Dr. O'Brien talked Mrs. H. into letting him select some families from our records to study. Seems Doc's curious about the subject of family diagnosis and has some ideas on it himself."

"What *hasn't* he ideas about?" interjected Molly. "Long as I can remember, Doc has collected hobbies the way other people collect stamps. Let's get to work, time's a-wasting."

"What an addlepate I am," Kitty cried with instant remorse. "To work, to work!" She buried her head in the papers at her desk and the room was quiet.

The morning set a pattern, Elaine found. There were the first few minutes of shop talk, grousing, teasing, and general chatter that ebbed and flowed with each new tide of phone calls to doctors, clinics, patients, hospitals, welfare people; a comparison of notes on similar cases and progress; occasional consulting with Frieda about a chronic invalid or a talk about paranoic symptoms in some patient; a discussion of ideas for a campaign on safety in the home to present at a conference; the making out of assignment sheets and a gradual drifting away to the day's cases or to work in a maternity clinic or a child-care clinic. At the end of the day the nurses and Phil would come in to write their reports and plan for the following day, and follow up with any necessary phone calls.

There was a pattern but no rigid routine. Sometimes a nurse went directly to a case without first coming into the office, leaving her schedule sheet to speak for her. Or she might be too busy with cases to report in for the afternoon, and paper work would have to be saved for the following day. Monday afternoons were reserved for staff conferences, which all the nurses attended, with Phil, Mrs. Hagstrom, Dr. O'Brien, the nursing supervisor, and sometimes a Board member or a specialist. Once in a while there were county-wide meetings or lectures to attend, and as many nurses went as could be spared; at the next conference there would be reports to keep everyone abreast of the latest developments in the smoking and heart-lung cancer controversy, the last bulletins on the efficacy of the Salk vaccine, new approaches in public health . . .

At the end of the week Mrs. Hagstrom called Elaine into the office for an informal assessment of her progress in learning about the staff, their duties, general policies, and procedures.

Next week she would have to meet representatives of the organizations she would have dealings with, from the Community Service Office to County Welfare, the Boys' Club, the Senior Citizens' Club, hospital personnel, and the County Health Department.

Evidently satisfied with Elaine's quickness in grasping these essentials, Mrs. Hagstrom outlined plans for the coming week. Elaine would observe at the clinics and begin visiting patients with each nurse.

"I know you're eager to be on your own," Mrs. Hagstrom smiled. "These first days always seem to be a marking-time period, but truly they're not. You must have this groundwork and a period of observation before getting assignments of your own. Don't think we're not every bit as eager as you are. The nurses have been overloaded since your predecessor left." She gave a rueful shake of her head. "We've prided ourselves on having a very low turnover here in spite of the fact that nurses persist in getting married and retiring too fast for us to replace them. Usually our nurses have settled down in this area and have returned to their work after having children, say six or seven years later. They know how desperately they're needed. But our last two girls married men from the West Coast, and here we are, shorthanded. Well. So much for that."

The telephone operator, doubling as receptionist, opened the door.

"Mr. Yaeger's here, Mrs. H. Shall I ask him to wait?"

"Oh, please ask him in."

"Is that the new consultant?" Elaine began, and then halted, wondering whether she should have acknowledged Kitty's rumor.

But Mrs. Hagstrom laughed. "The grapevine's in good working order, I gather. Not a consultant but an observer. We'll see what kind of arrangements we can make, what records he'd like to use, what families he'd like to visit, and so on. Stay and meet him."

There was something familiar about the husky tone of the voice in the anteroom that said, "Thanks, don't bother to show me in."

When Dirk Yaeger appeared in the doorway, ducking his head to pass under the low frame, Elaine groaned inwardly. What an inauspicious start! If only he could have been an absolute stranger instead of the Galahad of the station who had offered her a ride.

It would have to be, she thought, depressingly aware that she had snubbed him. She would have liked to slip unnoticed through the doorway behind him, and postpone the meeting until she was flanked by other members of the staff to provide at least a little anonymity. But Mrs. Hagstrom was saying, "I'd like you to meet the newest addition to our staff, Elaine Forrest, who comes to us from a Chicago hospital. Elaine, Dirk Yaeger."

He must have been surprised when he swung around, but there was no trace of discomfiture as he held out his hand and said hello. "We meet officially this time. So you're a nurse."

Childishly, she prickled at that. "What did you suppose, a teacher or a waitress?"

Undisturbed, he said, "What a curious bracketing—to be parenthetical. No, I thought—oh, possibly a model or a visiting Junior Leaguer."

He had a way of putting her on the defensive, of setting her teeth on edge for no particular reason. There was nothing in his words to give offense—on the surface they even seemed flattering—but behind the apparent compliment she detected a concept of her that was far from flattering, a dismissal of her to the decorative and nonutilitarian areas of life, for which he probably had little use.

34

It was a challenge, and by the time he finished explaining to Mrs. Hagstrom about their short encounter at the station, Elaine had recovered her savoir-faire enough to be distantly cordial to him. "I'm awfully glad to meet you—officially. Now I must get back to my apprenticeship. I'll see you Monday at the meeting, Mr. Yaeger."

Monday morning Elaine spent at the clinic with Miss Schwartz and Kitty. A volunteer weighed each prospective mother, noting dates, names and preliminary material on the cards before ushering her into the nurse's office for further interviewing.

How was she feeling? Did her ankles and feet swell? Was she eating well, not gaining too much weight? Any vomiting or nausea? Was she managing all right with the other children? Not lifting too much? Getting enough sleep? How did her husband feel about the coming baby? Was he worried about finances or did he look forward eagerly to the new child?

Then the volunteer aide brought the mother to the doctor's office for examination. Elaine was surprised at the variety of types and the range of economic brackets. On the heels of a ragged little Italian girl who was having her first baby at eighteen came a well-dressed young woman in her thirties; after her a large Negro woman who worked in a hospital and expected to continue until a few weeks before the anticipated birth. Then a middle-aged woman with her husband, refugees from the Hungarian revolution.

Elaine listened, admiring Kitty's effortless way of imparting information while she seemed to assume knowledge of the patient, admiring her skill in raising the patient's morale or encouraging her to maintain good nutritional habits.

The last was a pretty, short-haired blonde girl in a yellow

maternity jacket and plaid skirt. Kitty pulled out the girl's card and smiled.

"No headaches again? No swelling? Sleep well? Why, this is getting monotonous. Weight still good? Fine. How is your husband doing in his new job? Well, you shouldn't have too many financial worries with your hospitalization now . . ."

Kitty closed the last folder with a sigh. "That's it for today. Miss Schwartz, would you join us for lunch at the hospital coffee shop?"

"Thank you, Kitty, but I have an errand to do before the conference."

Kitty and Elaine slipped on their light jackets. "All right. See you this afternoon then."

"Rather a dour type, isn't she?" Elaine commented on the way to the hospital. "I guess that's the most gracious thing I've heard from her lips yet. She must like you."

"Maybe. She knows I like her."

"You do?" Elaine was surprised. "You're such radically different types that I don't see what common ground you have."

Kitty gave her a sidelong glance and laughed. "Don't sell her short and don't be misled by her manner."

"But it's so ungracious that I don't see how the patients can help resenting her."

"Did you watch them this morning?" Kitty asked. "Notice their reactions?"

Elaine confessed that she had been too fascinated by Kitty's deftness to heed what was happening at the other desk in the room.

"Thanks for the compliment," Kitty murmured. "I'm not slow, but did you notice that Miss Schwartz interviewed at least three or four more patients than I did? And with no sacrifice of information either, I assure you. She doesn't relax in her manner; she's perfectly formal with each patient, rather remote in fact, and yet they never show any resentment. I think it's because they sense that she knows her job so well that they place absolute confidence in her. They know they couldn't be in better hands. And the doctors respect her too. Look, there's a table by the window." She dashed for it like a terrier and plunked down her bag to reserve it. "I'm going to splurge and have a salad and dessert with my sandwich."

They brought their trays back to the table and sat down in the September sun.

"It still puzzles me that you *like* her. I can understand admiring her professionally but she seems so unlikable to me."

Kitty shrugged and bit into her sandwich. "I suppose it began with professional admiration for her skill and integrity and then—oh, it sort of spread, and in a way I feel sorry for her too. She's so alone, but there's never a suggestion of pathos about her." Reflectively she added, "I suppose when you grow up with a large family, as I did, you have to learn to like and respect different types. Dad always said you mustn't be finicky either with food or with people." She speared a lettuce leaf on her plate and grinned. "Not that I'm equally fond of all my brothers and sisters. I lack the impartiality of angels."

"I never knew anyone from a large family," Elaine said. "Most of my friends were only children, or had at most one or two sisters or brothers."

"Lucky you, no cast-off clothing to wear. My youngest brother is still wearing a leather jacket Mom bought for my oldest brother for his birthday before Dad was killed; and Colleen has just now outgrown my first evening dress. I sent her twenty-five dollars to buy a brand-new one for her senior prom this year. Can't blame her for wanting one. Mom has been bringing the old one up-to-date for the last eight years. Last year she dyed it and that was the end of the trail. Colleen called it Methuselah."

Elaine drank a glass of milk, a little shocked at the casualness of Kitty's reference to her father's death. At home Elaine never mentioned her mother, though her portrait hung over the mantelpiece and there were photographs of her from the Seymour Studios. She always had the feeling that it would be too distressing for her father, that one simply didn't thrust the melancholy thought of death upon him.

But then Kitty seemed casual and nonchalant about everything. Look how she joked about her childhood and what seemed to Elaine abject poverty. Could she be superficial, insensitive, unfeeling? It didn't fit in with what little Elaine had seen of her. Well, it would have to be pursued another time.

"Was Dr. O'Brien a friend of yours in Chicago?"

"He's been our family doctor for several years, and I guess he was one of my father's closest friends. Dad was awfully put out with him for deciding to move back here."

"Was it Doc who suggested applying here?"

"Yes, and he can be very persuasive. He drummed in the fact that public health nurses had to take a good deal more initiative and responsibility in their work than most nurses, and of course that appealed to me."

"And you would like the independence too," Kitty surmised.

"Yes. But there was something else besides, a personal reason."

"You mean beyond the reputation of the Kahopac V.N.A.?"

"Oh, the fact that it's one of the oldest and best of the nursing services attracted me, naturally; but the personal reason is that my mother used to live around here." Elaine gave a funny, deprecating little laugh. "Not that it means much, but I suppose a sort of curiosity lured me on since I know so little about her. Perhaps I had some idea that I might meet someone who knew her, could tell me more about her—not very likely though—

she must have left Kahopac twenty-five years ago at least. Goodness, it's late! We'd better get back for the conference."

"Gosh, yes!" Kitty drank up her coffee, finished her doughnut, licking her fingers like a child, and scrambled into her jacket. "Let's go."

CHAPTER FOUR

The conference was already in session when Kitty and Elaine arrived and quietly took chairs behind Phil Roland and Frieda Manship.

Dr. O'Brien had already introduced Dirk Yaeger and was listening, thumb and finger plucking at his little Vandyke beard, while Dirk was explaining his presence at the V.N.A. conference.

". . . not only a question of studying the records you have on hand, with Mrs. Hagstrom's permission, but a matter of visiting patients and observing firsthand perhaps a dozen families over a period of time to make what is called a family diagnosis."

"I'll bet that's just a newfangled way of saying, Use common sense," Molly Carew said. Elaine guessed that she was ready to bristle and battle with Dirk, but his smile disarmed her.

"Exactly. It's really a pretty oldfangled method that general practitioners have used for years, and it's something that you nurses who are used to dealing with an individual in the framework of home and family are also familiar with and grasp very quickly. A nurse accustomed to treating a patient isolated in a hospital bed isn't as well equipped by her experience to understand it. It's not an easy concept to put into a few words, but let me try."

He jotted down some notes on a pad of paper, tossed down the pencil, and glanced around the room. "I don't have to tell you that the physical factors are not the only elements of an illness that you have to deal with. You've all had cases where patients stayed sick long after they should have recovered, and sometimes you must have had patients who recovered faster than you expected. There are all sorts of stresses that affect both a patient and his family—emotional, financial, social, vocational—and these stresses are important for us to consider because they often provide the clues to a quicker and more effective recovery—or to a better adjustment if the illness is chronic—for everyone involved. You're all probably familiar with one or two families in which everything always seems to go wrong, often without any apparent cause. Morale is a tremendous factor, and basically we're trying to discover how to jack up morale. To do this we have to understand what the family's problems are and how each individual fits in."

He nodded toward Frieda. "Social workers are concerned with this problem too, and I'm sure Miss Manship has given you help in this direction."

"I think he's very nice," Kitty whispered to Elaine. "I won't mind taking him along as observer."

"Sometimes one person's illness can make the whole family disintegrate," Dirk continued. "Now of course we can't have flying squads of psychiatrists to treat these conditions, which are beyond our scope; but you nurses have some of the general practitioner's opportunities to observe and learn and apply your knowledge, and to call in other community resources to aid a family in trouble. If you learn to evaluate such conditions, you may be able to forestall all sorts of trouble by bringing in outside help before it's too late."

Pausing, he shoved his hands in his pockets. "You may be wondering what business this is of a social scientist. Frankly, I don't think the thesis committee would have okayed this subject if I hadn't also majored in psychology and done some field work in this area under the direction of a psychiatrist who is deeply interested in this subject. He pointed out that if we can learn more about these factors, which promote a healthy and fruitful family life, we're on our way to dealing with the increasing problems of mental health, juvenile delinquency, alcoholism, dope addiction, and some of the other ailments of our society. We want to give the children of these families a better start and perhaps rescue some older people from chronic invalidism."

Suddenly he grinned and looked around the room. "Good heavens, I didn't mean to embark on a lecture. I feel as if I'm bringing coals to Newcastle."

"I like his manner," Kitty said *sotto voce* to Elaine. "He doesn't talk down to us just because he's in a different field, and yet he makes everything perfectly clear and acts as if we can teach him a few things."

"Just a technique," scoffed Elaine. "He's not a psychology major for nothing. Can't you see he's soft-soaping us? I'll bet he's calculating the effect of every word."

Kitty looked perplexed. "You sound as if you have a grudge against him, but I don't see why."

"Nothing of the sort." Elaine flushed. "Why should I? It's just that I don't intend being taken in by his lounging around, acting so casual and full of humility. Look how he made Molly Carew melt. But it didn't work on Frieda; she sees through him."

". . . would love to hear more," Mrs. Hagstrom was saying, "and I'm sure later conferences will offer instances in illustration of Dirk's remarks. If you have any questions, you're invited to talk to Dirk after the conference. Meanwhile there are quite a few cases we have to consider here today. Mr. McKinley, the amputee, is first. Doctor, I've been wondering if we're not justified in insisting that he be fitted for braces. Phil thinks there's a good chance with a little training to make him more independent . . ."

Miss Schwartz, Elaine noted, took little part in the conference. Too much of a lone wolf, perhaps. It surprised her, though, that Frieda was so silent. She kept her eyes on her notes, scarcely venturing a word unless she was directly questioned, merely sitting poker-faced in her armchair in front of Kitty. Idly Elaine speculated on the cause of such a taciturn manner, but it was only when Dirk Yaeger leaned forward a few minutes later to comment on a case that she caught a clue. In those few seconds Frieda lifted her eyes and stared at him across the room with a queer, sullen expression. Was she jealous? Maybe she thought Dirk's study trespassed on her realm. Maybe she resented him as an outsider and an interloper. Come to think of it, she was the only person who hadn't heard Kitty announce the news of another observer, so perhaps it was simply a momentary annoyance at not being informed earlier.

Frieda was by nature an outsider, Elaine thought with a touch of sympathy. Those thin features, the deep-set eyes, the tightly drawn braid of hair, the long neck—all combined in an effect of gawkiness not readily conducive to a personable appearance and manner. Yet she dressed well in a subdued way and was irreproachably neat.

How different Frieda was from Kitty, who could wear a ten-dollar dress in the most enchanting way and who had a knack for finding good lines in cheap clothes. This, Elaine was an expert at evaluating. How different, too, from Miss Schwartz, who was an outsider on her own terms, so that there was no sense of exclusion. There was no question but that she chose aloofness and privacy with all awareness of the penalties they inflicted.

Dirk, too, she suspected, was by nature an outsider, but he had the ability to bring himself into any circle when he chose. She knew it because she recognized the same faculty in herself—

or fancied she did because she had always been sought after, was always the one who could choose.

Poor Frieda. Poor, proud Frieda.

She felt Dirk's eyes on her and bent her head to take notes.

Elaine was beginning to have the comfortable feeling of knowing her way around—not only geographically in the town and its environs but in the workings of the staff and what would be expected of her now that she was beginning calls on her own.

And the room was her own. Her instinct had been sound in this selection after all. She had been able to maintain her privacy. Occasionally Mrs. Flandrau breakfasted with her but more often in her own room. Cora chatted while serving Elaine her juice, eggs and bacon with buttered toast, and coffee. One morning she asked if it would be all right to vary the menu at times. Elaine said she would be pleased, and thereafter had the pleasure of surprise dishes—a mushroom omelet or French toast or a mysterious concoction in a small casserole made with chili powder, eggs, tomato juice, cheese, and chives.

"Delicious," she exclaimed, fanning her mouth, "but hot— I'm dying for a glass of water."

Her appreciation delighted Cora and she asked if Elaine needed any mending done, any ironing or other little chores? Soon she was caring for Elaine's wardrobe in an efficient way that the maid at home never had done.

Mrs. Flandrau, Elaine found, was a remarkable person. She rarely opened a conversation on more than a "Such beautiful fall weather; did you have a good day?" level unless Elaine herself sought a little relaxation. Yet she always seemed to welcome talk, and Elaine found herself beginning to tap on her door for a nightcap of conversation. Elaine later learned that the old lady not only read voluminously—Cora's shopping trips to town always included a visit to the library—but corresponded with a host of friends all over the world. It was astonishing how the woman took an interest in almost any subject that arose, and was generally better informed than her young guest.

"You never know whether the topic will be a revolt in Indonesia or the state of agriculture in Mexico. She's quite likely to have heard only recently from a consul in Peru or a banking official in Stockholm. You'd love her, Bryce," Elaine wrote.

"But when are you coming to see me? Next month, I hope? Contrive a business trip if you must have an excuse, since last week end didn't work out. And you must meet Mrs. H., as everyone calls my boss, and Kitty Gullen, who has become my closest friend here and is eager to meet you. There's so much to tell you about, my new cases, etc. Come soon or I'll blackmail you with silence. Todd O'Brien has been asking about you too."

She hummed as she dropped the letter into the mail slot, and smiled at finding a letter from Bryce in her post-office box. She raced through it before going out to the car that had been supplied by the county and would be hers while she was on the job.

"Your father is looking fine . . . glad to hear your work is progressing and you're making new friends . . . Do you see much of Todd O'Brien? Hope to see you in two weeks; there's something I'm anxious to talk over with you, so let's not plan any double dates, hmmm?"

Short and crisp, like most of his letters. Elaine knew he disliked writing, but anyhow he was coming. She had a moment's misgiving. Maybe he wanted to talk again about getting married at Christmas. She must make him understand that it wasn't practical until next year at least. But that she could take care of when he arrived. He was always so reasonable.

45

"Bryce is coming in two weeks," she announced to Kitty as she sat down at her desk that morning. She flipped the letter open for Kitty to read. "I'm so anxious for you to meet him. Let's arrange a double date with one of your boy friends."

Kitty looked up from the letter. "But he specifically asks you not to, Elaine."

"Never mind, don't worry about Bryce's objecting," Elaine said confidently. "As long as we can be alone part of the time he won't mind."

"What do you think he wants to discuss with you?" Kitty sounded dubious. "I'd like to meet him, Elaine, but really I'd rather postpone it till his next visit."

"I told you not to worry, it'll be all right. He probably wants to set a date for the wedding, that's all, and I'll have to talk him into postponing it again. Now what's the matter?" Laughing, she tipped her chair back and balanced it on two legs. "Disapproval sticks out all over your face. I know. You think I'm a contriving, managing woman. Maybe I am, but he loves it and I don't think it does anyone any harm. I know Bryce, he'll end up being delighted. Come on, don't be a spoil sport, Kitty."

"All right then, I guess you know what you're doing. You usually do. I'll see what kind of male I can scrape together for a date, but both my regulars are out of town."

"They're nice boys," Elaine said, turning back to her desk, "but I think you could do a lot better if you cared to."

"Better than——? Oh, I see what you mean . . . I think. You mean, why settle for a shoe salesman or a real-estate agent when there might be someone in a higher echelon around, say a lawyer or a doctor? That it?" Kitty shook her head and chuckled. "You know, considering how opposite we are in background and ideas, it's surprising how well we get along. I suppose I'm just not ambitious, either for myself or my prospective, let's hope, husband. Until I find my altar ego I'm willing to settle

46

for enjoying dates with nice young men who aren't any more serious than I am, but who can talk well about a fair range of subjects, who like sports and going to movies and plays or just dancing or strolling. Laissez-faire is my policy. I'm not going to try to steer someone else's life. I figure I'd better learn more about my own first. If I meet that altar ego and fall in love, it won't be with the idea of changing him. I won't like it if he tries to change me either, I might add. End of lecture."

As an afterthought she added with an elfin grin:

> " 'The man she had was kind and clean
> And well enough for every day,
> But, oh, dear friends, you should have seen
> The one that got away!'

Credit Dorothy Parker."

"Break it up, break it up," boomed Phil, clapping a hand on Kitty's shoulder. "Don't you two ever get tired of hen sessions?"

Obediently Elaine whirled around and hunched over her records. "Yessir, yessir, please don't flog me, sir." In a stage whisper behind her hand she said to Kitty, "Won't see you tonight. I'm having dinner with Doc and his wife."

She went back to making up her schedule for the day, consulting the list Mrs. Hagstrom had made up for her and the case records in folders from the files.

Mrs. Rogers: bathe, give Vitamin B-12 injection.

Kenneth Tolheimer: change wrist bandage.

Mrs. Hansom, diabetic patient. This was a more complicated case and Elaine read through all the records in the folder. Lives with daughter and son-in-law and grandson, erratic in health, history full of relapses, at one time lived alone in apartment; after severe attack moved in with daughter. Some stress in home

47

but daughter apparently devoted and eager to help. However, more signs of stress in husband and child, especially in alcoholism and compulsive eating. Daughter refuses suggestion of nursing home for mother.

Perfect setup for Dirk Yaeger's family-diagnosis thesis, probably. Elaine made a wry face. She didn't intend to ask for any suggestions; she'd rather handle a case alone, without an observer, particularly at the outset.

Only three cases for her first solo day. Mrs. Hagstrom was certainly starting her off gently, but that was evidently office policy. Elaine checked through her bag and went out to her car. It pleased her to be able to find the way to the Rogers' house without inquiring directions.

She parked in front of the house, strode up the walk between the two pine trees, and rang the bell. It was a brown frame house with muddied red shutters in an unprepossessing neighborhood. There was the sound of children shrieking, the whir and clatter of a tricycle, footsteps pattering down the stairs. The door was jerked open and a slatternly little woman pushed back strings of hair.

"You're the new nurse?" she hurried on, "Thank goodness you've come. Gramma's been giving us such a time. She's getting worse and worse, needs more attention than the children, won't take her medication, won't let me wash her face, and she's getting awfully sloppy. Tommy, clear away that trash and let the nurse by. Liza, pick up that doll, I mean it now, pick it up. This way, Miss—uh."

Elaine followed the woman upstairs, not supplying her name because the woman was too disorganized to care.

"Gramma, here's the new nurse. Now be nice to her, Gramma, and do like she says. If you need me, yell," Mrs. Rogers said to Elaine. "I've got a stew going and have to run downstairs. Up and down, up and down, all day long. Bathroom's down the hall, if you can get her to take a bath."

"Good afternoon, Mrs. Rogers," Elaine said to the older woman composedly in the face of a ferocious scowl. She opened her bag and laid out paper towels on the dresser while the woman plucked with blue-veined white hands at the light spread and muttered unintelligibly to herself.

"Can you hear me all right, Mrs. Rogers?" Elaine approached the bed with cotton for cleaning the arm. "If you'll roll up your sleeve we'll have this done in a jiffy." Then she jabbed in the hypodermic syringe with Vitamin B-12 and it was done.

"Sure. Think a person's deaf?" The voice matched the belligerence of the expression. "Can't see as these shots do any good."

"They do," Elaine assured her. "How would you like a bath? It's been so warm this week it would make you feel nice and fresh. Now don't scold. I'll help you out and into your robe after I run the bath."

The bathroom was a gaudy, flowered blue but the towels were white and clean and the tub spotless. When the water was steaming into the tub she went back for Gramma and found her cackling triumphantly.

"Fooled you, didn't I? Got into my robe myself, see?" But she leaned heavily on Elaine walking down the hall.

Elaine folded a towel and helped Mrs. Rogers sit down on a corner of the tub with her back to the wall for safety. She washed the wrinkled, blue-white flesh, carefully folding a large bath towel around her as she finished so the old woman wouldn't catch cold. She dressed her in a clean nightgown and helped her back to bed.

When she returned from washing her hands, the old woman was lying back in the bed and Elaine rearranged the pillows to make her comfortable.

"Thanks," Gramma said gruffly. "If my daughter-in-law weren't so helpless I could have a bath more often. Incompetent nitwit."

"With the children and housework and cooking and bringing you meals she's probably pretty busy," Elaine said indifferently. She snapped her bag shut. "Well, I'll see you next week about the same time."

As she turned to leave, Mrs. Rogers said suddenly, "What's your name, girl?"

Elaine halted at the doorway. "Miss Forrest."

The old woman beckoned and Elaine came reluctantly back to the bed. She mumbled, "Sorry—you know—about grumbling. You *will* come back, won't you?" and bent an anxious, pale-eyed stare on Elaine.

"Of course. It's my job, you know."

Gramma plucked at the spread. "I know. But . . . never mind." She waved Elaine away. "Goodby."

Hardly a very interesting first call, Elaine reflected as she opened the car door. But at least she hadn't driven around the block four times to get up nerve to go in, as Kitty said she had done on her first solo call, and announce herself with quaking knees and quavering voice as the nurse from the V.N.A. But once in, Kitty had stayed two hours.

A young mother ill with flu had been lying on a couch unable to keep track of her two toddlers, racked with anxiety about their adventures but too weak to do anything but cry. Kitty had fetched the children, blocked living-room exits, washed the dishes stacked in the sink, tidied the place, made beds, found a box of toys to amuse the children, and made some soup for them and their mother. Before leaving, she had phoned the neighbor, a plump, elderly matron who was only too happy to bustle about and help out.

On hearing about the episode, Elaine had been appalled at

spending so much time with one patient, especially on chores that had nothing to do with nursing.

"I don't look at it like that," Kitty had retorted, curtly for her. "There's no telling how long it would have taken her to recover if someone hadn't helped out and given her a chance to feel like a human being instead of a sopping, helpless mass of worries and misery. Her husband telephoned me that night. He had just returned from a sales trip and wanted to thank me 'for all I'd done for them.' A quick recovery and two new friends and what did it cost me? A couple of hours of chores."

"But you could have been making two or three other calls," Elaine had argued. Kitty had calmed down and said, "Wait till you've been here two months. The number of cases handled isn't the only guide post and goal."

At the next house Elaine had only to change the bandage on a broken wrist, and half an hour later she stopped in front of a yellow frame house in a nice neighborhood a little beyond the town limits. The Thompson house was the only one that didn't look fresh and well tended. The lawn was frowsy with weeds; the unclipped bushes were full of awkward spikes and sprouts; the few remaining flowers had wilted on their stems. One of the shutters hung awry and the porch roof was sagging. Elaine side-stepped a big gash on the porch steps.

The woman who came to the door was rather like the house, once pretty but now somewhat frayed and frowsy. Her house-dress was pinned at the neck, her belt was worn, there was a rip visible in the seam under the sleeve.

Her manner was well bred, rather sweet, apologetic as she invited Elaine in. "I hope you'll excuse the way the house looks. With an invalid it's rather hard, you know . . ." Her voice trailed off. "This way upstairs is Mother's room."

She led Elaine to what must be the best bedroom, the largest and certainly the best-kept room. The sun pouring in through the south windows tinted the pale blue walls almost green. Mrs. Hansom lay propped against two pillows watching a quiz program on TV.

"Here's the new nurse, Mother," said Mrs. Thompson brightly. "Her name is Miss Forrest, dear. Now won't you be good about taking your medicine?" she said coaxingly. "Can I help you with anything, Miss Forrest?"

Elaine asked a few questions about diet and medication, and knitted her brows at the answers. No wonder the old lady looked "tuckered out," as Kitty would say. Both diet and medication were irregular. Apparently the daughter used cajolery in vain and lacked the spine to insist on medication at the proper times. Elaine read them both a lecture on the stern necessity of this. From what Mrs. Thompson had in the refrigerator she prescribed the meal for the night.

"Hey, Mom," came a voice from the bottom of the stairs, "this all the milk we got left? Aren't there any cookies?"

Mrs. Thompson gave Elaine a harassed look and moved to the door. "Billy, you know I don't like you to scream up the stairway; it hurts your grandmother's ears and it's very rude. Come up here if you want to talk."

"Oh, Mom," a pained but resigned voice answered. "Oh, all right." The reedy voice was in startling contrast to the clomp of heavy shoes on the stairs, but Elaine was hardly prepared for the sight of the boy. He was pale, moon-faced, and moon-shaped; everything about him seemed globular, from the round blue eyes to the blob of nose and the full, red-lipped mouth. Never had she seen a boy so grotesquely fat for his age and height. Now she remembered the term "compulsive eater" in the case history, but that hardly seemed a strong enough term.

He said hello nicely to Elaine but to his mother he went on complaining until, exasperated, she told him to take fifty cents from her purse for milk and cookies at the store.

"Don't forget to ask Grandmother if she'd like something too," she reminded her son. He obligingly did and met with a surly no. "He's a good boy," she said when he left. It was as if by ignoring his abnormality, she wiped it out of existence.

Downstairs, Elaine reminded Mrs. Thompson that she must be inflexible or her mother's diabetes could not be kept under control, but watching the woman's evasive eyes, she guessed there would be little change. With a sigh she opened the door just as Mrs. Thompson's husband walked in.

He doffed his hat politely and Elaine noted his handsome features—large blue eyes like the boy's, thin well-formed nose, slightly full lips, and a head of curly blond hair.

"Hugh, what are you doing home this early?" his wife exclaimed. "You haven't—haven't . . ." Her voice trailed off and she darted a look at Elaine that was charged with embarrassment. "Hugh, come in, don't keep Miss Forrest waiting in the door. She's the new nurse, Hugh—my husband."

There was nervousness in her manner and now Elaine could see why. His eyes were bloodshot and there was enough whisky on his breath to make her suspect that he was drunker than he looked. Quickly she said good-by, repeating that she would be back next week.

Once in the car she breathed more fully. What an atmosphere, how oppressive, how it seemed to choke them all. It must stem from the invalid mother. She really belonged in a nursing home where she would be under strict medical care.

She gave her head a shake. She didn't intend to get into the habit of carrying all her cases with her, as the others did. In the middle of dinner Kitty might suddenly hit on an idea to improve the self-sufficiency of a crippled patient.

Nevertheless her depression was hard to dismiss. Elaine curved the car onto the main highway and stepped on the gas, the faster to escape the Thompsons.

She considered what dress to wear to the O'Briens' that evening. The pale blue jersey with short sleeves and full skirt? No, the flame-colored cotton shirt, so beautifully tailored and yet so feminine with its versatile neckline, and the cummerbund and skirt of warm chocolate brown, with coral necklace and earrings. Much better for fall.

Speculating on the evening ahead raised her spirits, and she wondered if there would be other guests. There had been little time so far for relaxation and she would welcome meeting some nonprofessional people for a change.

CHAPTER FIVE

"I wouldn't have believed it," Elaine exclaimed at sight of Connie O'Brien that evening. "I simply couldn't picture you in the country, but now that I see you here it's hard to imagine you anywhere else. But you still have the look of a marquesa, only a marquesa in tweeds instead of silks. Ever the last word in fashion wherever you are."

"That's it," cried a girl on the couch in front of the fireplace, and turned to a tall man standing by the fireplace. "Isn't that what I said, Paul, a marquesa?"

"Countess, you said," Paul corrected. "Close enough."

"Elaine, I'm so pleased to see you again. And in case you're homesick, the Serrills are from Chicago too. Katie, Paul, this is our latest Nightingale on the staff of the V.N.A., Elaine Forrest."

Paul was frowning at Elaine in a puzzled way and suddenly snapped his fingers in triumph. "I remember now! The picture on Frederick Forrest's desk. You must be his daughter. I remember his speaking of you when I interviewed him a couple of years ago for a story on Chicago lawyers of the past. In fact, Todd, you were the one who arranged the interview," he reminded Dr. O'Brien.

"That's right. And didn't Katie photograph him for the series?"

"Oh, that's one of my favorites, Mrs. Serrill. You caught just the sort of eagle look that I like about him."

"Awfully glad you liked it. Paul and I did several features together for the paper."

Elaine liked the looks of the Serrills. Katie had delicately pretty features with a sprinkling of freckles over her nose, with alert blue eyes that warned you not to overlook her quietness. Her husband, perhaps eight or ten years older, had a rakish twinkle in his eyes and a more worldly look. They had moved to Kahopac so that Paul could accept a job on a New York paper and he commuted by train. Katie had not decided yet whether to look for a job or do free-lance photography; they were still getting acquainted with the area.

"They live near you, Elaine," Doc said. "The old white house just below. You might not have noticed it because it's screened from the road by the woods."

"Oh, but I have. I can see it from the window of my room and it looks charming."

"You must come to visit us," Katie urged her. "It's one of the oldest houses around here, and we have a lot of what must have been the original furniture."

There was a ring at the doorbell and Doc opened the door for Dirk Yaeger. Disappointing, Elaine thought. She had hoped to meet new people, and could have done very nicely without Dirk's company.

"I've seen you before," he said promptly on meeting Katie Serrill. "Weren't you at my aunt's barn one day? Aren't you the photographer who is doing a picture story about the barn?"

"Oh, you mean Annie Dunne's barn, yes! It's the most fascinating place in town—out of it, I mean. Dr. O'Brien told me about it and I've been hunting through the barn off and on for a week with the idea that there might be enough material to make up sort of a history of the town."

"I wouldn't be surprised," Dirk said, sitting next to her on the couch. "When I was a kid I used to poke through that loft, and found every imaginable kind of document, all sorts of clothes dating 'way back, old scrapbooks, daguerreotypes, skin-covered trunks, furniture—all kinds of treasures. I remember a church book with records back to the year seventeen-ten, marriages, births, deaths, sales of land, donations to the church of pigs, goats, chickens, milk—you know, instead of a salary to keep the pastor going. I suppose it started because her father was mayor of the town for several years and became quite an authority on local history, even wrote monographs for the Historical Society. People used to clear out their attics and send over everything they didn't need on the chance that something might prove valuable."

Connie said, "Todd, that's what we can do with those trunks and things from our attic. I hate to interrupt, but the maid tells me the roast is ready and mustn't be kept waiting. Please come into the dining room."

At the table the talk turned to medicine. Paul was doing a feature story on epidemiology, the science of treating epidemics, and Dr. O'Brien dipped into his variety of experiences during his World War II medical assignments. He made the tracking down of diseases seem like medical detective stories, which involved the tracing of a pinch of dust, a fungus, a jar of mushrooms, and a pair of travelers on a bus who left a wake of smallpox.

"What a subject for a dinner party," Connie O'Brien finally complained. "Paul, I insist that you do your research with Todd in his office or I'll be worrying about the mushrooms in the sauce. Dirk, tell us how your research is progressing."

"You might find that equally depressing," Dirk smiled. "So far I'm concentrating on reading through case histories in preparation for choosing some for closer study." At Katie's inquiry he went on to explain more about his objectives.

"It sounds fascinating," she exclaimed with infectious enthusiasm.

It irked Elaine a little that Dirk directed so much of his talk to Katie, and on impulse she mentioned the Hansom-Thompson household as a possible subject for further research. At once she was annoyed at herself for seeming to invite Dirk's interest, the more so because he remained cool and rather detached about the suggestion.

"It's something I'd like to look into," he said politely and turned back to Katie. A glint in his eyes hinted to Elaine that he was purposely annoying her with a show of indifference.

All right, if he wanted to play it cool, she could too. After listening to an exchange between Doc and Paul Serrill on the subject of maturity she joined in.

"People today stress environment and circumstances so much, it makes me wonder if we don't undervalue individual character. I think the final responsibility lies with the individual, not with the social climate or the schools or the parents." She had the satisfaction of sensing that Dirk had stopped talking with Katie and was listening to her.

"Don't you think that the individual has a better chance to realize himself if he has a favorable start?" Dirk asked mildly from across the table. "I don't see that it helps to permit a handicap to remain if you can remove it. Are you just possibly biased because you're enjoyed a fortunate start?"

Elaine flushed angrily. Of course things had always gone well for her. She had always had friends, admirers, had done well in school and in her work, in sports, in whatever she undertook. But she was sure she would somehow have done pretty well even if she hadn't had such advantages. That much she could not gracefully say and instead she retorted, "Don't you think you would have managed quite well whether you were given advantages or not?"

"She's got you there, Dirk," Doc chuckled. "No one can say you started with any favors dealt to you. You pretty much scrambled to get your education, working your way through college and graduate school, and I fancy you'll make a good life for yourself."

Dirk's eyes were fixed on Elaine in that startling blue gaze of his that left her discomfited even when she considered that she had scored on him. "I think I will," he said with a little smile. That irritating self-confidence again!

"Curious," Paul Serrill said thoughtfully, "how habits and patterns build up in a person and would seem to be predictable, inflexible—and yet you can never tell when there might be a breakthrough into a pattern very different, sometimes much better. I remember a professor of mine from the Chicago slums whose older brother was killed in a gang fight. Yet another brother became a detective in a special squad working to combat and prevent juvenile delinquency."

"Like the sound-barrier breakthrough, you mean?" Elaine queried. "Only this is a moral barrier? Maybe there's a chance of a breakthrough during childhood and adolescence, but I can't see much chance of it in an adult."

"It needn't take the form of a moral barrier," Dirk remarked. "It might be, oh, an emotional barrier, say."

"That's the endless mystery of human beings," Doc broke in, leaning forward over his plate, with his little beard bristling with eagerness. "That mystery is something I feel at every delivery. To hold a baby in your hands, whatever the environment and circumstances, and to think how impossible to predict what will pass in the next decades to shape that life . . . I suppose that every time I have delivered a baby there has been that moment of wonder—what kind of life am I helping to bring into the world? What are its potentials? Good, strong, weak, evil—great? What?"

"Come, dear, let's have coffee in the living room," Connie said, rising briskly from the table.

Doc tugged at his beard. "You see? Whenever I wax philosophical or eloquent, there's Connie to prick me back to my ordinary humble status."

Dirk moved through the door to the living room behind Elaine. "You certainly take a gloomy view of human development," he observed. "Does it jibe with your idea that the individual character is the shaping force?"

"It's a consistent force, so it's not likely to change much," she retorted.

"Well, it's a subject that can't be dismissed with a few remarks," Dirk said, drawing up a chair next to hers. "Like to have dinner sometime and talk about it?"

She opened her mouth with every intention of refusing, but instead said sweetly, "My fiancé is coming to visit me soon. Maybe you'd like to have dinner one night with us and Kitty Gullen."

If she had hoped to embarrass or disconcert him, she didn't succeed. He took out a pipe, lit it, puffed a few times, dropped the book of matches on the coffee table, and said simply, "Glad to. Let me know when he's coming. By the way, if I'd known you were coming here tonight I'd have offered to pick you up."

"In your little Plymouth?" she said derisively.

The unruffled blue gaze turned full on her. "Oh, you remember my chariot from the station? Horrible sight, isn't it? Would it embarrass you to be seen in it?"

What a way he had of turning the tables on her. Now it was a challenge, daring her to be snobbish about it, and she could only say, "Of course not. I've no doubt it's very reliable."

Two weeks later the train pulled into the station just as Elaine parked her car. As soon as she saw Bryce descend the train steps she called out and moved toward him with a wave of her hand. He kissed her and she patted the shoulder of his topcoat possessively.

"How good you look!" she exclaimed. She snuggled her hand into the crook of his arm and led him in the direction of her car. "Darling, it's grand to see you. Until this moment I didn't realize how much I'd missed you. How's Dad? Tell me about things at home."

"You look as beautiful as ever," Bryce said, smiling.

"I've made reservations for you at the hotel, the nicest room in the place. It faces east and gets the sun all day from the south windows and there's a lovely view of the town."

Bryce patted her arm. "Just as efficient as ever, aren't you, Elaine? You're not working too hard? Your dad is fine but said to tell Todd O'Brien he hasn't forgiven him yet for deserting him."

"Isn't that like Dad, to view it as a personal affront that Doc moved here? No, I'm not overworking, but I'm already making as many calls a day as any nurse on the staff. Oh, just throw your suitcase in the back seat."

She started the engine with a zestful roar and then let it idle a moment while she gave Bryce an appealing look. "Bryce, please don't be angry with me, but I have a confession to make. I know you wanted to spend this week end alone, but there are so many people I wanted you to meet that I couldn't resist arranging just a couple of evenings with friends. You don't *really* mind, do you, dear?"

He glanced away from her out of the window and she perceived that he was more provoked than she had thought he would be. Instantly she revised her tactics.

"You see, I thought if you truly didn't want to see them, we could cancel the other appointments."

"I have only two evenings here," Bryce said quietly without looking at her. "There is something important I wanted to talk over with you. Some other time I would like to meet your friends."

"Oh, well, of course I'll call it off then. Unless you wanted to talk this something important over now so we could be free later . . . No. Well, when we get back to the hotel I'll call."

"I would appreciate it." Bryce was himself again, not withdrawn but turning to her with his nice smile.

At the hotel she made a call first to Dirk's apartment, knowing he'd probably be out on calls with a nurse. No answer. Katie Serrill was out too, probably photographing or doing research at Annie Dunne's.

She came out of the phone booth, shaking her head ruefully. "Bryce, I'm so sorry but I couldn't reach a soul about tonight or tomorrow. Maybe tomorrow we can call the Serrills—they'll be terribly disappointed to miss meeting you—but I don't see how we can avoid a date tonight with Kitty Gullen and Dirk Yaeger. We'd made reservations at Leo's for dinner and dancing. Oh, dear, what shall we do?"

He sighed. "I suppose we'll have to go through with the one for tonight and just call off the one for tomorrow then. Thanks for trying, honey."

"Bryce, you *are* a good sport. Well." Unconsciously she had adopted Mrs. H.'s habit of clipping off a train of thought with that emphatic *Well*. "You'll want a shower and that will give me time to run home, bathe, and change. Then I'll pick you up here about seven and we'll drive out to Leo's to meet Kitty and Dirk. How's that?"

Bryce's face crinkled into a smile. "You just can't help

scheduling, can you, honey? You have your father's faculty for organizing things and you're stuck with it."

"Stuck with it?" Elaine laughed too. "Is it so bad?"

He gave her a kiss on the cheek, smiling. "No, it's not terrible. Run along. I'll wait for you on the veranda."

What luck that Bryce wasn't the stubborn sort, Elaine thought with satisfaction. Dirk would have been mulish about such a thing, she was sure; and she rather liked the idea that tonight he'd meet Bryce and would see why she felt so secure and satisfied with her life. For a moment it had looked as if her plans might be knocked into that old cocked hat, but now they were turning out well.

Kitty was late as usual, but it was comfortable to sit on the lawn in front of Leo's with Bryce, back once more in her thoughts to the life in Chicago so different from her life here. Back in a cozy threesome with her father and Bryce, chatting after the theater or back from a sail on Lake Michigan.

Bryce swung her hand gently as they leaned back in their lawn chairs and talked.

"Ever think about giving this up and coming back to Chicago with me right now?" Bryce asked. He shifted for a better look at Elaine.

"Oh, Bryce, not again? Are you sorry you encouraged me to be a nurse?" she teased him. "If I'd remained a parasitic debutante I would have been conveniently at home and we could have been married by now, couldn't we? But on the other hand you wouldn't like a parasitic debutante for a wife, would you? Now that I've started this, I want to see it through." More seriously she said, "Besides, it wouldn't be fair to Mrs. H. and the staff to break in another nurse on short notice, would it?"

The pressure on her hand tightened. "You're right, darling, I wouldn't want you to abandon ship. I suppose I just wanted

reassurance that you missed me. You always seem so self-sufficient, you know, that it's a little discouraging sometimes . . .
But what I wanted to talk to you about was a change in my
own plans——"

"Oh, here come Kitty and Dirk now. Kitty, over here!"

She waved and Kitty came dancing through the shafts of
light from the windows, a white butterfly with her white full
skirt flowing out. Behind her, looming dark in the pale light,
came Dirk with his yard-consuming, easy stride.

"Oh, Elaine, Bryce, do forgive me for being so late. Poor
Dirk was so patient with me. Elaine, this is *Bryce*?" Kitty's
warm voice spread an aura of magic over the name as she looked
up at him. Bryce was a little taller than Elaine, but he seemed
to tower over Kitty. "You're as handsome as your picture, but
somehow very different. I guess I expected more of a social
type—I couldn't be more delighted to be disappointed."

"I can't say that I'm disappointed in you," said Bryce gallantly, "and Elaine has described you so that even your short-
comings seem charming."

"What can you do with such a woman?" Dirk said resignedly.
"Only put in your sentence of waiting with good grace. But
it's so beautiful here under the stars, you can't have been too
impatient waiting. Look at those hills silhouetted against the
moon."

When they moved inside, Leo came smiling to greet them.
"Miss Forrest, Miss Gullen, how are you both? I began to wonder if you'd given up dancing and eating. Ah, how do you do,
Mr. Thorne, Mr. Yaeger. I've saved this table by the window
for you."

He pulled out chairs for the girls and motioned for his head
waiter while the moon stared through the window at them—a
Cyclopean orange eye.

Kitty had a way of making the simplest meal seem festive,

64

and tonight in the candlelight she was sparkling. The face that sometimes appeared a trifle too thin and pale glowed pink and her smile was more beguiling than ever. Music always filled her with rhythm and when the orchestra began to play, her eyes half closed in barely contained pleasure.

Knowing Bryce's indifference to dancing, Elaine was about to press his foot as a gentle hint when he forestalled her by turning to Kitty. "You look as if you love to dance, Kitty. Shall we?"

In an instant she was up and ethereally floating away in his arms. It was so untypical of Bryce that Elaine's eyes followed them in wonder. "That was considerate of him," she murmured, half explaining to herself. "He doesn't care much for dancing, but he is so sweet about sensing when someone else wants to dance."

That was true but tonight he hardly looked as if he were performing a reluctant duty. Elaine gave a small laugh to disown the flicker of disturbance and focused for the first time on Dirk.

"Dirk, how nice you look dressed up," she said involuntarily.

The white shirt and well-tailored suit set off the deep tan of his face, a contrast to his usual costume of slacks, sweater, and dark shirt. His face was too long, narrow, and craggy for good looks, but there was something compelling about it nevertheless. It was not handsome like Bryce's but it was unforgettable, not the kind of face that could easily slip out of memory. Even the crest of hair had been tamed a little. "For Kitty's benefit?" she said sarcastically. "I had an idea you two might hit it off."

From the gleam of his white teeth she knew Dirk was pleased at her reaction. "Slouch around long enough in slacks and shirt and you can always make an impression when you do dress up," he grinned, and she was suddenly conscious of how attractive he could be. Watching the dance floor in a lazy survey, he pulled out his pipe and automatically began loading it. "No, not for Kitty's benefit." He lit the pipe and drew on it, and little circles of smoke rose in the air. "Oh, Kitty and I do hit it off, but not the way you mean." After a moment he nodded toward the dancers. "If you want to see a couple hitting it off . . ."

Elaine followed his glance and froze. Then she laughed. "What are you trying to say? I'd be surprised if Kitty and Bryce didn't like each other. Why shouldn't they? You're not trying to make me jealous, are you? My goodness, they just met."

The little circles of smoke rose regularly. "There's something more than liking there, Elaine. There's some chemistry working there that's potent; you can tell just by watching them together."

From a distance she could see Bryce smiling down at Kitty, relaxing as he never had before on a dance floor. She turned her back on the sight decisively to demonstrate her confidence and said acidly, "They look fine together, but I've been told that Bryce and I make a handsome couple too, so what does that prove?" She looked directly at Dirk. "Tell me—don't you like him? Or are you trying to prove something? What is it? Are you just needling me for fun?"

He returned her look. "Bryce is not the man for you, I suppose that's what I'm trying to prove. As a matter of fact, I like him."

Elaine gave a short, incredulous laugh. "If you think Bryce would be disloyal . . . Well, really, I don't know why I even bother to . . . Oh, you're impossible—and it's none of your business anyhow!"

He looked steadily at her. "Don't be so sure it's not my business." There was a brief silence and then he stood up. "Come, let's dance." Even while she retorted that she didn't want to dance, he took her hand and, unable to free it without a fuss, she followed him, inwardly fuming.

At the dance floor there was a pause before the music resumed, and in that moment she was half minded to show Dirk that she wouldn't be coerced, that she had a mind of her own. The impulse sprouted so urgently that just as the music struck up again she suddenly twisted away at the very instant that his arm closed around her waist and swept her back to him.

It was a physical shock, the kind she had once felt in an elevator when she stepped in, expecting it to go up instead of down—but there was a strange kind of electricity in it too.

Speechless with anger at his blocking of her movement, she held herself as rigid as possible. She knew he was deliberately baiting her, confronting her with a choice between a public display of conflict, which was distasteful to her, and acquiescence to his will. She steeled herself to silent resistance, and to regain her poise she tried to watch the dancers around her, but she could not lose her consciousness of Dirk's arm holding her close to him whenever she strained away. And he was laughing at her!

"Relax," he said into her ear. "Can't you dance, or is it that you always, always, always want you own way? Do you ever consider that someone else's way might be better *once* in a while?"

Her inward rage mounted murderously. Why was he so determined to humiliate her? She'd show him she could dance! It took a few minutes to effect the transition, to free herself to the rhythm of the music, to force herself to relax in his arms, but when she succeeded the effect was extraordinary.

It was like melting into the music, like moving in some strange element altogether new to her, and the electricity came back and compelled her to lift her eyes to meet Dirk's and then shyly, unaccountably, to lower them again. She felt his hand draw hers close to him and then release it to stroke her hair and hold her face against his shoulder. He whispered her name and she moved in dazed bewilderment with him through a wilderness of music and new emotion. She was scarcely conscious of the ceasing music; it seemed to continue even while they stood waiting, and when it resumed there seemed to have been no pause.

CHAPTER SIX

When the music stopped at last and the players stepped down for the intermission, Elaine returned with Dirk to the table in silence. After a moment she noticed that Dirk had cupped his hand over hers on the table, and she moved to withdraw it. But he tightened his hold with a fierce grip that made her look helplessly at him.

"Please . . . I don't know what . . . I've never——" She was torn between wanting to put her head on his shoulder and cry and wanting to catch up her stole and run away and wait for Bryce to come and soothe her back into the life she knew all about. And there was the terrible concern, too, for Bryce if he should discover how these few minutes had transformed her into someone else, a person she never knew existed. This sort of thing didn't happen, couldn't happen, to her! She put her other hand to her head, and tears started in her eyes. Hearing Bryce's voice behind her, she snatched away her hand, reached for her purse, and walked quickly to the powder room. It was at least a temporary escape from her dilemma.

She sat looking into the mirror with her fingers at her lips, staring at the face in front of her with its wide, blue-tinged eyes, its startled thick, dark eyebrows, the nostrils in the straight nose flaring slightly, and the dark hair tumbled where it had been resting against Dirk's shoulder. She could feel again his presence.

She took out a comb and ran it slowly through her hair, powdered her face. Her lips quivered as she applied lipstick, but she pressed them together. At last she drew a deep breath and looked at herself again.

This was the real Elaine, carefully groomed, unswayed by any talk of chemistry. This was the Elaine who always knew what she was doing—not that silly, emotional, unpredictable creature of a preposterous situation. Enough nonsense about Dirk. He could not be trusted; he was probably practicing his psychology on her.

Still, a tiny thrill ran through her. Dirk might not leave the decision entirely in her hands . . .

The door opened and a face was reflected in the mirror. Elaine, still churning with uncertainties and immersed in her own thoughts, took a prolonged moment to place it as Frieda Manship's and to respond to her greeting. Somehow it was hard to recognize her in so unexpected a setting; she had always seemed to Elaine more like a neutral quality of a profession than an actual person.

Frieda sat next to her at the dressing table and combed her straight hair severely back in its precise coiffeure, showing the high forehead. "Lovely night, isn't it? I saw you dancing with Dirk and you both looked very absorbed, I must say. I waved and neither of you noticed." There was both pique and coyness in her glance at Elaine's reflection.

Preoccupied, Elaine said without conviction, "Oh, sorry." She reminded herself then that Frieda was on the staff and it would be wise not to display her edginess. "As a matter of fact, Kitty and my fiancé from Chicago are here too."

"Oh, that handsome man dancing with Kitty?"

Was there a touch of unpleasant innuendo in the words or was Elaine being oversensitive because of Dirk's remarks? Elaine couldn't decipher the bland face in the mirror. Frieda went on chattily, "Isn't Leo's a charming place? One of my favorites. I'm here with Dr. Trevelyan tonight."

The door opened again and Kitty appeared in the mirror. Overlooking Frieda, she said hesitantly, "Elaine, are you all right?"

Elaine swung around with a little smile. "Why, of course. Why not?" Her voice sounded very natural but she was annoyed at Frieda's presence. "How beautifully you and Bryce dance together. I think it's the first time Bryce has honestly enjoyed dancing."

"But he's very graceful, very relaxed," Kitty exclaimed in surprise at the implied criticism of his dancing. Then she noticed Frieda. "Oh, Frieda, for heavens' sake! I didn't know you were here. Hello, how are you?"

Her belated effort to be cordial did not appease Frieda. She said coldly, "I'm fine, thank you. I don't know why you're so surprised to see me here. I do eat and dance and have dates too, you know."

Kitty stared blankly while Frieda picked up a little gold bag and stalked from the room. "Well, of course you do, it's just that . . ." Kitty's voice trailed off at the slam of the door, and she turned to Elaine. "Well, I put my foot in my mouth that time, didn't I? I shouldn't have been so tactless, but what's she so sensitive about? She's always so touchy, so afraid of being left out. Oh, dear, I didn't mean to hurt her feelings."

Elaine dismissed Frieda with a wave of her hand. "Don't worry, she'll forget it by morning. . . . You seem to like Bryce." Her composure was back and the chimera of jealousy and suspicion was vanishing.

"He's *such* a nice person, Elaine." Kitty rested her chin on her hand and looked at Elaine's reflection. "You *are* very lucky, you know. He's not at all what I thought a man with a social

71

position would be like, but then you're not either, exactly. He's so absorbed in his work."

"Yes." Elaine dropped her comb into her purse and took a last-minute appraisal of herself in the mirror, searching for a reassurance that might never be quite the same again. "He might become quite a famous scientist someday."

"Scientist? But isn't he planning to . . . I thought . . . Oh, nothing." Slowly Kitty took out a compact and began powdering her face. "If you're ready to go back, don't wait for me, Elaine. I see some major repairs."

Elaine's confidence returned on the way back to the table. The whole episode was so absurd. Dirk meant nothing to her. How could he, what did they have in common? She knew almost nothing of his background except that it must have been totally different from hers; whereas Bryce had been brought up on the same social level, they shared the same friends and memories, had known each other for years, and could rely absolutely on each other.

She passed Frieda and Dr. Trevelyan and carefully smiled but did not stop at their table. Frieda would want to meet Bryce, and Elaine was not in the mood for such an encounter.

The men were deep in conversation, politics and education and world crises. A little peeved, Elaine decided that Dirk couldn't have been as emotionally involved as she had supposed. Yet his welcoming rise and glance at her held something particularly searching and intent, so that she felt herself flushing and avoiding his eyes.

"It will be a hard step to take," Bryce continued to Dirk. "Fortunately a lower salary has little importance for me."

"How do you feel about it, Elaine?" Dirk asked her.

"Feel about what?"

Bryce looked uncomfortable. "I hadn't gotten around to telling Elaine yet but Kitty thinks . . ." He stopped, as if surprised, and then cast Elaine an uncertain glance. "What I started to tell you earlier this evening was that—I'm giving up my research job and going into teaching."

"Oh, Bryce, you're joking," Elaine said lightly. Then in the silence that ensued she said, "You surely wouldn't do anything as foolish as that."

Both men looked at her. With abrupt discomfort she added, "I mean, you have a job that might prove very important someday. Why on earth would you give it up when you like it and have such responsibility and opportunity? That's silly. And just for teaching!"

Bryce took a long swallow of water. "I don't think it's silly, Elaine." The rebuke in his voice was plain and she smoldered with resentment of Dirk, who in some fantastic way must have had a hand in this. But Bryce's next words acquitted Dirk. "This is something I've been drawn to for a long time, Elaine. You see, I've become more and more aware of my limitations as a physicist; I know I'll never make any original contributions to the field . . ."

"Oh, how can you say that? It's too early to know."

He held his hand up and smiled. "I know. In this field the signs appear very early. By his twenties a physicist has generally shown the qualities of original thought that indicate an outstanding contribution, and I'm not kidding myself—I haven't. I love the work, but that's not my value." His enthusiasm was rising and Dirk, too, was watching her expectantly, which gave Elaine the uncomfortable feeling that she had lost control over Bryce, the situation was out of hand. "Elaine, I think that teaching is my real vocation, that I can excite youngsters about the field, get them interested, make them aware of the great need for scientists in every field. And when a friend of mine asked me to lecture in a couple of his classes, it was the experience I needed to convince me. It was a challenge I could meet despite his complaints about the lethargy of his students. This is the work I want, Elaine."

"But why couldn't you lecture without giving up your work? Why should teaching a few students matter so much? And how do you think you'd like the daily grind?"

"That is a drawback in every field, but if you love the work you can cope with it."

Dirk leaned forward with his eyes alight. "It's not simply a matter of 'teaching a few students,' as you say. Think back to your own high school days. How many teachers made you *think*, made you feel strongly? Were you working at full capacity? Most of us learned to get by on the least possible effort, on slipshod work. We didn't learn the joy of delving deep into a subject or working to unleash the knowledge that could be ours. This is vital work, Elaine!"

"We don't teach our students to value things of true importance: learning, loving the work, thinking straight, using creative imagination. Here we spoon-feed our students. In Russia they're turning out thousands of engineers and scientists while we give courses on charm and family relationships and concentrate on football teams!"

"Hear, hear," said Kitty, slipping into her chair. "What's everyone so excited about?"

"Here's a guy like Bryce with the ability, and the love, to become a fine teacher—and Elaine can't understand how important that is! She's trying to block him!" Dirk almost glared at Elaine.

"I'm not trying to block him," she protested. "I only want him to be sure, to take his time. I don't think he should decide offhand when after all it concerns me too."

"And you don't want to be the wife of a high school teacher!" Dirk shot at her.

Kitty intervened. "Dirk, that's not fair. You know that Elaine

74

would want whatever is best for Bryce," she said loyally, angry at his attack.

There was a silence while the waiters brought the next course. "Well, I didn't intend to throw a hand grenade into the conversation," Bryce said, trying to rescue the evening. A screen of conversation was duly erected to disguise the tension that had developed, but behind it Elaine was unhappily delving into her relationships with these three.

Kitty's readiness to believe only the best about her friends made Elaine examine herself more probingly. It angered her to be unable to throw off Dirk's accusation. Her motive was sheer selfishness; she did not welcome the status of the wife of a high school teacher. She caught herself up, forced herself to think of Bryce and his needs, but it didn't come easily. She resented the crushing of her plans. Privately she could acknowledge that she liked to run things and people, and even took pride in doing it well so that others were rarely conscious of it, but no one else had exposed her as much as Dirk.

Her resentment swerved to him. Why did he want to do this, to humiliate her, break her engagement with Bryce, damage her friendship with Kitty? How dared he claim to like her, much less to . . . But then he hadn't, had he?

At that moment Dirk's eyes turned on her, held her eyes with a gaze that made her breathe in sharply. What was it in his eyes —anger? Contempt? Pleading? Something else she could not fathom?

In any case she must avoid him; there must be no repetition of this evening's strain. What she knew of herself told her that she must be in control of situations, and she had the uneasy conviction that Dirk would never allow himself to be controlled. It was her good fortune, she soothed herself, that Bryce was reasonable, amenable to suggestion.

That night she was troubled by dreams. She was drifting in a canoe with Bryce on a lake; suddenly the canoe began floating faster, faster, and they approached a river, turned into the river with increasing speed, and were tossed among rapids and rocks so that at every moment she was ready to shriek at new dangers, new whirlpools . . . She started, heard the ticking of her clock, felt hot, and flung off one of the blankets. It was hard to return to sleep.

Then she was in a fencing match with Bryce; they parried and lunged and just as she was about to call *touché*, her opponent disarmed her, and when he tore off his fencer's mask it was not Bryce at all but . . . And then she herself was Kitty and it ended in a swirl of confusion.

She awoke unrested and dressed reluctantly. There were minute lines shadowing her eyes in the mirror, and she met Bryce in a state approximating bad temper. But when they drove over to have brunch with the O'Briens, their welcome began to restore her spirits and she enjoyed Doc's bursts of enthusiastic talk and Connie's scoffing, fond, down-to-earth attitude toward her husband.

Then a pleasant drive in the warm October sun out to the house to meet Mrs. Flandrau and Cora and see her room and the house and its environs. They stayed for a late tea while their hostess entertained them with stories of friends and travels.

Bryce bent to look at the photograph of the dark young man on the mantelpiece. "He reminds me of someone . . . Hmmm. He could almost be a younger version of your father, except that his coloring is so different. Did you notice, Elaine?"

"It does look a little like him."

"That's Carlos Milliet," Mrs. Flandrau said. "His parents were my dear friends when we lived in Argentina. When he came to school here he used to spend many week ends with us. More tea, Bryce? Elaine? For a while I thought he might

76

stay here. He fell in love with a local girl but was called back to Buenos Aires because of the death of his father."

"Why didn't he marry the girl?"

"Oh, I believe her family didn't want her to live so far away, and he had to stay in Buenos Aires to manage his estates. It's years since I've heard from him except for Christmas letters, but he's always been one of my favorites."

Elaine left them and went upstairs to change into another dress for the evening. Though she was curious about the Serrill house and eager to have Bryce and Kitty meet her new friends, she dreaded the possibility of another clash on the subject of teaching. There was something incendiary about Dirk that was catching, and she didn't like being a minority of one.

Instead of driving, she and Bryce walked down the hill, enjoying the last splashing of color by the sun on the leaves. The hills heaved with red and gold still, but the bare patches on northern hilltops where the leaves had fallen gave notice that few more such beautiful fall days remained.

Katie and Paul saw them walking up the lane and met them at the door. It was clear from their joy in showing off the house how much they loved it, and Elaine could understand why. The rooms were large, and great beams ran the length of the living-room ceiling; the fireplace was large enough to walk into. The walls were pine-paneled and there was a huge bay window overlooking almost the same view Elaine had from her room. There was a feeling of coziness and warmth and solidity.

A crunching on the gravel driveway advertised the arrival of Dirk's Plymouth. When Kitty and Dirk came in, Katie's exuberance barely waited on introductions. "Oh, Dirk, what do you think? Remember my telling you about my idea for a picture story, 'A Barnful of History'? Well, I talked to the editor of the *Clarion*, and he wants me to do a series in text

77

and photographs based on Annie's barn! What do you think of that?"

"Wonderful, Katie! Just make sure that my aunt doesn't have some wild notion that she's entitled to whatever you make on the deal."

"I told her I'd print up any photographs she wanted, and that seemed to satisfy her."

Elaine relaxed. Tonight she could watch Dirk quite objectively and wonder what caused her to exaggerate the effects of that experience the night before.

The moon hung full on the horizon after their buffet supper, and Paul suggested that they make the best of the warm evening on the terrace. The men set up the lawn furniture and Elaine leaned back in her chaise longue.

"How quiet it is here," Kitty said softly. They listened to the remote sounds in the woods, a twig snapping, a movement of trees in a rustle of wind, a dog baying in the distance. From the highway came a whirr of tires on the road and a flicker of headlights reached through the woods.

"Ever thought of living in the country like this?" a voice spoke next to Elaine. Dirk had taken the chair next to hers.

"I'm a city girl," she answered positively. "I like tall buildings and the movement of people in the streets and the bustle of the city. Oh, I enjoy spending our summers in Michigan, but that's different."

"I know, nice to visit. That's what I feel about the city. But wait till you've been here a while; you might feel differently. Someday I'd like to settle in this area. I've even found the site I want."

Something in his voice made Elaine stir uneasily. "Bryce and I will probably rent an apartment in the city, but sometime I suppose we'll move to the suburbs."

Out of the short silence came a quiet, "Doesn't that depend a

little on where Bryce teaches—assuming that you let Bryce go
into teaching?"

There was that everlasting needle. "You needn't talk as if he
were a robot in my hands," she retorted angrily. She shivered.
"Bryce dear, would you fetch my stole from the living room?"

"You have a very attentive suitor," Dirk observed as Bryce
went into the house.

Scenting derision, she bridled. "He happens to be courteous
and thoughtful, but he's no marionette, if that's what you're
implying."

"I agree with you. *I* don't think he's a marionette, I think
he's a man. And one of these days you'll find he's in revolt
against string-pulling, however devoted he is."

Elaine sat up straight. "How you have the nerve to . . ."
Bryce's figure crossed the lawn to the terrace and she lay back
in the chaise as he came up to her with the stole. "Oh thank
you, Bryce."

"How is the Thompson-Hansom case coming along?" Dirk
inquired, puffing on his pipe.

"All right," Elaine said shortly.

"Is that the case you spoke of to Dr. O'Brien this morning?"
asked Bryce, sitting by Elaine's feet on the chaise.

"Yes. We were discussing whether Mrs. Hansom should be
sent to a nursing home. I think her daughter would pay more
attention to her family and things would straighten out."

"Why don't you arrange it if it's that easy?" Dirk said lazily.

"Well—I—it's not the kind of thing that can be done in a
hurry. They have limited funds . . . sometimes they don't even
have the dollar or two for our calls and— And . . ."

"And?"

"Well, Mrs. Thompson doesn't seem to favor the idea . . ."

"Maybe it's not so simple," Dirk said. He lowered his pipe.

79

"I've been looking at their records. It looks like an interesting case. Mind if I go along with you one of these days?"

She did mind but could not legitimately object.

"Look!" Kitty spoke in a whisper.

A shape detached itself from the woods and cautiously moved toward the evergreens near the terrace. Paul switched on the terrace light and a doe with a brush of white tail stared at them, hypnotized under the glare. For a moment it stood a-quiver on slender legs, then wheeled and bounded out of sight.

"For all the world as if she wanted to join our party. How Dad would love that," Kitty said with a soft chuckle.

"Is your father a naturalist?" Paul asked.

"Dad? No, a pilot, but he loved animals and was always bringing us pets—a raccoon, a kinkajou, a chameleon. He died years ago," she added, understanding that her use of the present tense had left a misapprehension. "I'm sorry to sound confusing, but I've never gotten out of the habit of thinking of him alive. He was away so much, you see, that I've never lost the feeling that he might walk in on my next trip home."

The quiet invited her to continue; the soft night kindled an attentive, gentle sympathy in the listeners. "I know it must sound silly," she said hesitantly, "but I still feel very close to him. You know, he used to write lovely long letters to keep in touch with us and—well, we still have them, and even now I read them sometimes and I keep discovering new things that I didn't understand as a child."

"What a wonderful way to remember him," Bryce said gently.

Paul took his wife's hand and she settled herself against him on the chaise they were sharing. Instead of disapproving of such an illusion and voicing some skeptical comment, as Elaine would have expected him to, Dirk had rested his head on the back of his chair and was staring up at the stars, almost wistfully, she thought. It crossed her mind then that he had been orphaned as a boy.

Tendrils of memory of her mother reached out insubstantially to Elaine, the fading memories of a child with limited understanding and no basis for interpretation. "I wish I had something like that to treasure," she murmured half to herself, "something to make me feel I knew more of my mother than I do . . ."

She became aware that Dirk's head had turned toward her. His hand stretched out across the little space between them and she moved suddenly, just enough so that he withdrew it. There must be no more of that electricity. She felt vulnerable, and regretted having said anything.

Kitty had heard too. "Didn't you say your mother came from Kahopac, Elaine? Why can't you find out more about her here?"

Elaine forced a light laugh. "Oh, there's little chance of finding anything, I know so little about her. Only her maiden name —Phyllis Logan." She stirred restlessly, too conscious of Dirk's nearness. "It's probably a silly idea anyhow. What does it matter now? Bryce, I had no idea it was so late. If we don't leave now, you'll miss that early train tomorrow. Katie, I hate to break up your lovely party, but we must go."

Dimly the words penetrated her mind as she heard Bryce say to Kitty, "Perhaps we'll meet again, Kitty." Her scalp prickled as it had when she entered the hospital with her father for that operation, as it had the day her mother fell into a delirium. She pushed the words out of her mind.

But Sunday morning the words drifted back in spite of her, as she and Bryce stood on the platform waiting for the train. Pride would not permit her to mention them, but Bryce himself explained the context, without any suspicion that it had troubled her.

"Kitty told me that her brother has a law office in Chicago and has been urging her to visit him. I said if she comes, by all means give me a ring or drop me a line and I would show her around a bit." He frowned. "I've been thinking . . ."

Elaine's heart gave an abrupt lurch.

"Elaine, why don't you try to find out something about your mother, as Kitty suggested? I have an idea it would—mean a lot to you."

Elaine let out her breath again in relief. Her anxious glance assured her that Bryce was merely observing a courtesy in his invitation to Kitty, that it meant nothing beyond that, that as always it was Elaine he was concerned with.

"There isn't much information to go on. And I'm afraid it would only be depressing, Bryce."

"Couldn't your father tell you something that would be helpful?"

"He hardly knew her people. She was studying in Chicago when they met and I think he met her parents only once, when he came here for the wedding. I'm sure he wouldn't remember and, besides, I wouldn't feel right, asking him. It would distress him so. You know he never speaks of her."

"Yes, I know, even after all these years. But it does seem strange that you know so little about your mother."

"Well, I was only twelve when she died, Bryce. How much do most children know about their parents? Vaguely where they've lived; sometimes they know the grandparents, the aunts, uncles, cousins—but my mother was the only child and there are no relatives I know of to tell me more. I know only my father's side of the family and they're all rooted in Chicago."

The train whistle sounded through the valley.

Tentatively, feeling her way, wondering if Bryce could still be dissuaded, Elaine spoke of his plans for teaching. "You know I want you to go on with them if you truly think it's best, but do consider it carefully, won't you, Bryce?" She slipped her arm through his in search of their old comradeliness. "It was a lovely visit and I can hardly wait till you come back. Soon, do you think?"

"I can't say when I'll be back, Elaine; it depends on so many things." He kissed her as the train wheezed and puffed into the station, picked up his bag, and walked to the nearest entrance with his arm around her shoulder. "I'm glad that I met your friends after all, Elaine. I liked them so much. Good-by."

When he waved to her from the window of the train she waved a good-by, threw him a kiss, and was conscious of a queer wrench as the train pulled out. She watched the train disappear around the curve of the hill, and puzzled over the depression that was settling down on her now that Bryce had vanished from sight.

CHAPTER SEVEN

By Monday morning Elaine had shaken her gloomy mood. Before dressing, she leaned out of her window in sheer enjoyment of the warmth of the sun on the house and hill. It was one of those glorious days when merely driving from one call to another was a vacation, a bonus of time. She laughed at the sight of the big collie from the Serrill house playing with Mrs. Flandrau's orange-colored angora cat near the fish pond, tumbling around and yelping with excitement like a puppy instead of playing his proper role of the dignified, long-nosed patrician he affected to be.

In the usual office prattle and bustle Elaine hummed while she prepared her schedule and chattered to Kitty about the prospect of her first day at the maternity clinic.

"Cat got your tongue—to coin a cliché?" she said merrily to Kitty when it dawned on her that Kitty was uncommonly unresponsive and morose. Her teasing provoked only a pale smile.

"Aren't the Serrills a charming couple, Kitty? You liked them, didn't you?"

Kitty focused her eyes rather vaguely on Elaine. "Yes. Oh, yes. I liked them." She went on packing her bag.

"Hey, Kitty, you're forgetting your towels. What's the matter?"

Kitty looked at the towels on her desk. "Oh. Stupid of me."

She stuffed them into her bag and added like an automaton, "The party was fun."

Elaine studied her. "Your eyes look glazed, Kitty. Are you running a temperature?"

"No, I'm all right. Just tired. I didn't sleep well last night. You don't have to take my temperature and put me to bed, thanks." For Kitty the tone was downright snappish.

A little hurt, Elaine, who would have suggested that, turned back to her desk without another word. Once at the maternity clinic, she was busy and the episode quite slipped her mind.

The first patient was easy, the same girl Kitty had laughingly complained was so monotonously healthy and free of ailments and difficulties.

"A new patient, Miss Forrest," the volunteer aide announced, but before she could go further, an impish face peered around the door.

"Surprised?" It was Katie Serrill's freckled face, and Elaine jumped up with a delighted exclamation.

"Katie! What wonderful news! Why didn't you tell me Saturday night?"

"Oh, there was so much else to talk about, and when you mentioned you would be in the clinic today I couldn't resist surprising you."

She had known about it before her departure from Chicago, but had been too occupied with getting settled in their new home to report to the clinic until now. Yes, Paul was tremendously excited, could hardly wait till spring. So far she had gained only three pounds and hoped to be able to wear her usual clothes for another month or more. Yes, she felt fine, no nausea. She had been reading about natural childbirth and Dr. Spock like mad in preparation, and was faithfully doing exercises and learning to relax.

Elaine gave her some leaflets on diet and general health and told her to report back in four weeks for her next appointment. "In your eighth month it will be twice a week. Oh, Katie, I'm so excited for you. Wait till Kitty hears. I don't think she suspected either."

Elaine loved the work at the maternity clinic in spite of the pressure and haste. Most of the women were buoyant and happy about the expected baby. When occasionally a prospective mother appeared nervous and worried about her first baby, it was satisfying to console her with the reassurance that nature on the whole had dealt very capably with the problems of birth for millennia, and that the inconveniences of pregnancy would be more than compensated for by the baby. Elaine even enjoyed the occasional presence of a prenursery child or two who sometimes accompanied the mother.

She came out the clinic one noon to discover that the sky was overcast and a cold wind was cutting across the valley. So much for fall; winter was in the air now. The temperature must have dropped fifteen degrees in a few hours.

"Miss Forrest, Miss Forrest!

One of the volunteer aides called her back. The office had phoned about an emergency; none of the other nurses was available—could Elaine possibly handle the call?

Elaine scribbled down the address and got into the car instead of stopping for lunch at the hospital. All she knew was that a telephone operator had received a call from some man who sounded terribly ill, too weak to give details, and she had notified the office. It might be an accident, a heart attack—there was no way of knowing.

Following the directions brought Elaine into a winding dirt road a few miles north of town, and she watched for the mailbox with the name "Monsanto." She found the name on a curiously contrived box shaped like a miniature castle. Dubiously she drove up the paved driveway and emerged from the thick woods into a hillside clearing in the center of which stood a full-size replica of that incredible mailbox. It was a castle, fully equipped with turrets and towers, with everything but a moat —a fantastic sight in the New York setting. Surely this couldn't be the place. It looked closed and unfriendly, with no sign of life. If some eccentric recluse lived here, he would at least have a servant or two; but not a soul answered the door when she lifted the huge brass knocker. The wind was howling now—she felt as if Heathcliff might at any minute step around the corner of this Gothic monstrosity.

Impatiently she ran down the steps and took a path that led around to the back and spotted a garage that could house half a dozen cars, and a barn across from it that were smaller duplicates of the castle, both also of stone. Perhaps someone lived in an apartment over the garage; one of the windows was open. Sounds came from the barn; she had a vague idea that they might come from horses.

There was a door on one side of the garage and when no one answered her knock, she opened it and went up the dark stairway. The door at the top of the stairs was partly open, but something blocked the way and she barely managed to slip in sideways. At her feet lay a man crumpled on the floor, with his heavy shoulders wedged against the door.

Stooping, she examined him swiftly and found him burning with fever. Somehow she managed to half drag, half carry him to a couch a few feet away, and heaved him up on it so that he lay face upward. There was a two- or three-day growth of beard on his face and bruises around the eyes; his flannel shirt was torn. He must have fallen at least a couple of times.

In the bedroom off the living room she pulled a blanket from the bed and brought it back to cover him. The unshaven face was blazing hot; the fever must be alarmingly high. Her

87

thermometer registered 104. There was a telephone on the desk —she decided to try Doc first. He was in his office, thank heaven, and she made her report. Above the sound of her own voice she could now hear delirious mutterings from the couch.

"He's terribly weak, seems mentally confused, if not delirious, and has a temperature of a hundred and four—no, no coughing," she said rapidly, keeping her eye on the man. "I thought I'd sponge him with alcohol before you came, give him fluids. Can you come right over? Do you know where the Monsanto place is? Sort of a weird castle in the woods—yes, that's it. This man is the only one here. He's in back of the house in an apartment over the garage . . ."

"That must be Matthew Crawford, the groom and caretaker. The Monsantos are away in Italy for a year or so. Look, give him the fluids and sponge him and I'll be there in twenty minutes; you're on the right track."

Elaine closed the window. Through the open door of the kitchen she spied a broken cup on the floor near a splash of brown fluid. He must have tried to get himself some coffee, maybe when he staggered to the phone. She took a towel and the bottle of alcohol from her bag and turned to find the man's eyes open, fixed on her in a burning stare. He was mumbling something and she knelt down by his side. "Horses . . . water . . . feed . . . thirsty, thirsty . . ."

She brought him a glass of water but he pushed it away. "No, no. Horses first . . ."

"Mr. Crawford, you're a very sick man, I have to take care of you before I think of the horses. I'm going to sponge you with alcohol to bring down your fever and then——"

His eyes were glazed and he was feverishly insistent, angry at her. He tried to get up and she pushed him back firmly.

"You can't get up—you must lie still!"

He groaned and dropped his head back on the couch, rolling

88

it from side to side. For a moment she thought he had fainted again with the effort to rise, but he opened his eyes again and gripped her hand. "You've—got to—feed them. Three—scoops, Urchin, loose stall. Others—two."

"But, Mr. Crawford, I have to take care of you first——"

He rolled his head violently. "No! Horses . . . nothing—two days. Can't you—understand? Feed them!"

Obviously it was impossible to care for him until he was reassured about the horses. There was nothing for her to do but tackle it herself to prevent him from trying to stagger down in spite of his condition.

"All right, I'll go. Don't try to talk, I'll manage somehow and I'll come back if I need more directions."

"Urchin . . . three . . ."

"Yes, yes, I understand. Don't talk, just lie still and I'll be right back."

It had begun to sleet. She ran across the courtyard toward the barn, wishing she had worn a coat instead of a jacket. Only a little light fell through the barn windows, but she heard the horses whickering and plunging in their stalls, and finally found the light switch. One, the loose one in the big stall, must be Urchin.

She found the bins of grain but decided she had better water the horses first. She lugged several pailfuls and then began with the scoops of grain. They drank and ate eagerly, swishing their tails, moving their ears nervously in her presence. Ruefully she thought it was a good thing she had worn a uniform to the clinic; her dresses and suits were not exactly designed for farm chores.

Upstairs again, she found that Matthew Crawford had relapsed into a delirium and she began to sponge him with alcohol in an effort to bring down the fever. When he revived a little she fed him some fruit juice from the refrigerator.

When she assured him the horses were taken care of, he smiled weakly and fell asleep.

Doc's little Volkswagen hurtled into the driveway below and pulled up with a screech of brakes and gravel. He came up the stairs two steps at a time, gave the patient a quick examination, and listened to Elaine's succinct report, which included a sheepish reference to her barn chores.

He nodded with a grin. "I know this guy . . . you couldn't very well do anything else, he's very strong-minded—bullheaded is a better description." He pulled thoughtfully at his beard. "Temperature's down a degree, so I think he's over the worst. Looks like a case of Asian flu—you remember, after those cases on shipboard a few weeks ago we were warned of the likelihood of an epidemic. I think this is our first taste of it. It can hit hard, but most patients won't have too bad a time."

"Does he need to be hospitalized?"

"Not if someone can come to stay with him and keep an eye on him so he won't do anything rash, and see that he's fed, warm, comfortable. Tell you what, help me get him into the bedroom, then we'll see if he has any ideas about a relative or someone to stay with him. Better than getting a nurse because he'll be weak for a long time and he's less likely to tackle his work too early."

Crawford was a heavy man, but together they managed to get him into his bed, though Doc was breathing heavily. "Good body mechanics," he said approvingly to Elaine. "You know how to use your body to support and carry."

She grinned at him. "I can thank my sports training and a good instructor for that. All right, I'll stay with him until a neighbor or someone can come in."

While she waited for her patient to wake up, she straightened up the living room and kitchen, peeked into the pantry and refrigerator to find out what provisions he had, and washed the dishes in the sink and on the kitchen table. Then she squeezed some oranges and put a glassful of juice into the refrigerator.

The man had Spartan but surprisingly elevated tastes for a groom or a caretaker. There was a long shelf of recordings; on the walls hung three or four paintings, not reproductions but originals, and several shelves were packed with books. Strange to find all these in such a place. On a table in the corner chessman were set out ready for a game. What an astonishing groom Crawford must be.

There was a sound from the bedroom and she went to the door. "Feel achy? You've been running a very high fever, but it's beginning to subside. Don't try to talk much, but listen. The doctor said you don't have to go to the hospital if someone can stay here with you for a week or two. Do you have a relative or a neighbor who might help you out?"

The man shook his head and groaned at the movement.

"There must be someone. No relatives at all? Well, it might be simpler to send you to a——" She stopped, startled by the sound of steps outside. It was dark now and she did not relish the idea of an unknown visitor. Rather uneasily she went to the door with a quick glance around to see if there was a poker handy if it should be an intruder. Not that there was likely to be any danger, she assured herself, but she was nonetheless relieved to spot a potential weapon at the fireplace; this was a lonely and deserted spot.

She switched on the hall light and opened the door. "Who is it?"

A man carrying a large bag of groceries was mounting the steps and stopped abruptly. "Good heavens! Elaine, what are you doing here?"

"Is it——? Dirk Yaeger, what are you . . . ?" Suddenly she

collapsed against the wall with a fit of near-hysterical giggles. "What in the world are *you* doing here?"

"I came to visit Matt Crawford . . ." In alarm he exclaimed, "Has he had an accident? Is he all right? In the dark I didn't recognize your car."

"He has the Asian flu, but I think he's past the worst of it. Here, I'll put these in the kitchen if you want to say hello to him; he's awake now."

As she was starting to put away the groceries Dirk came into the kitchen with a grin stretching straight across his face. "I'll be darned. To come here for an evening with Matt and find you."

"Is he a friend of yours?" she said in utter amazement.

"Gosh, yes, for years. Matt's the one who rescued me from being a young tramp, got me started in reading, made me go to college. If it hadn't been for him . . . What in thunder is that?"

"What?"

He was staring at the top of her head. "I don't believe it."

"Oh, I suppose my hair got touseled when I was . . . feeding the horses . . ." Her voice trailed off self-consciously and she turned beet-red.

He plucked something from her hair and involuntarily she smoothed it. "Hay! You mean you were down there forking hay and feeding Urchin and the rest? Ill be——" With a sudden shout of laughter he swept her into his arms and lifted her into the air. "Who would have thought that our proper Miss Forrest would deign to play nursemaid to a bunch of horses? What a sight that must have been!"

Dumfounded by his reaction, Elaine began to laugh too until it dawned on her that the situation was a little out of hand. She stiffened in his arms and his laughter ceased. As he set her down on her feet in silence, she could feel his heart pounding through his shirt and sweater. Breathless now, she pulled back, half afraid to look up, but he held her longer, as if to show he was in charge, then released her slowly, staring down at her.

Feeling very small and strangely limp, with an effort not to stammer, Elaine said in a strangled, husky voice not at all like her own, "Your friend . . . I haven't . . . found someone . . . to stay with him." If she ignored it, it would be as though it hadn't happened, she thought.

Still staring at her, he said quietly, "You won't admit it even to yourself, will you?"

"Admit what? What are you talking about?" Her laugh didn't sound convincing to her either and she started to brush past him, but he caught her arm and she took a step back against the refrigerator.

"You know what I mean," he said steadily. "Face yourself for once, even if it doesn't suit all your plans. Improvise a little. Be guided a little by your emotions, don't be afraid of your heart. You don't have to plot your whole life, you know. It's not a medical chart; you don't have to make a prognosis. Suppose you did fall in love with me? It wouldn't be the end of the world for you—or for Bryce either. Suppose you did have to change some of your ideas about life—would that be so bad? I tell you Bryce is not the man for you. *I am.* And you know it if you'll only let yourself—I *know* you feel it too. Why are you so afraid of facing it?"

"I think you're crazy." Elaine's eyes fell wildly on the kitchen clock. "It's almost five o'clock and I've got to report to the office. Let me go!" Angrily she broke away. She dialed her number with shaking fingers, but composed herself to make her report.

"You can say I'll stay with Matt until he's better," Dirk said from the kitchen.

When she came back, he had emptied the grocery bag, and a large sirloin steak was laid out on the table.

93

"Good heavens, you can't give him that," she exclaimed. "Besides, he probably won't want anything but fruit juices and soup."

"I didn't know he was sick when I came," he reminded her drily. He weighed the steak in his hand. "Far too much for one man to eat. Why not stay and have dinner with me here? I daresay you have a pressing engagement."

It was exactly what she had opened her mouth to say, but he pricked that balloon. There was an ironic twist to his mouth, a mocking look on his face that set her on her mettle. He put down the steak, reached into his pocket for a tobacco pouch, and very deliberately loaded his pipe while he watched her. He struck a match and held it over the bowl. "In case you're worried," he said with the pipe clenched between his teeth, the mocking look still on his face, "I'll keep hands strictly off. Well?"

She flushed. "Don't be silly. I'm not worried. I've always been able to take care of myself. All right, I'll stay. I'd just as soon keep an eye on Mr. Crawford until his fever is down a bit more anyhow."

"You're not on trial; you don't have to make excuses for staying. Do you know how to set a table? Don't snap, I just asked. You'll find the dishes in that cupboard and the silver in the drawer; the mats are in the corner. If you can peel potatoes, you'll find them in the pantry. I want to see Matt and then I'll start dinner."

Unreasonably irritated at his assumption that she was useless in the kitchen, Elaine hurried to set the table in the living room, then got out the potatoes, peeled them, set them on the stove to boil, and waited triumphantly for Dirk to return from his talk with Matt Crawford.

When he came into the kitchen he removed the lid from the

pot of potatoes. "You don't want them boiling over," he reproved her. "Did you salt them? I thought not. All right, suppose you sit over there and talk to me while I make a salad and prepare a vegetable."

"How about French green beans with a sauce?" Elaine had to show him—if she could only remember what Cora had said about that recipe for the sweet-sour sauce.

"Go ahead, sounds fine." He smiled at her grim expression, but she was too intent on her task to notice. He busied himself with the salad and dressing and seasoned the steak, then sat back to smoke while she stirred her concoction on the stove. She hardly listened while he talked, but a few things came through. Dirk seemed to feel strongly about Matt, talked of his painting, his expert performance on the recorder—she had observed some sheet music around—his love of books, his interest in science. Since his return to Kahopac, Dirk had visited Matt regularly for an evening of talk and chess and listening to music, anything from Brahms and Prokofieff to "The Rain in Spain Stays Mainly in the Plain." She had to remind him it was time to broil the steak.

It was a good dinner. But the sweetest moment came when Dirk tasted the green beans and sauce. He lifted his eyebrows and looked distinctly surprised, though all he said was, "Well, you do have a way with beans. Anything else in your repertoire?"

Matt's temperature had dropped another degree, and before they ate he had some soup though without much relish, then he lay back half dozing, watching them through the bedroom door, until they finished dinner. They did the dishes together and Dirk was exasperatingly finicky about tossing back a plate or fork that had the merest speck clinging to it.

"You are——" Elaine set her lips firmly closed.

"Impossible," he finished cheerfully. "Want a game of chess or don't you play?"

"Yes, I play," she snapped.

"Let's have a game with our coffee then. It's done now." He poured out two cups and carried them into the living room. He brought the chessboard out and gave Elaine choice of white or black.

Puffing on his pipe, he opened with the moves of a scholar's mate. Wordlessly she thwarted him with her knight. From her expression he got no clue as to the deliberateness of her move. The game went on and Elaine played a purely defensive game, watching for a chance to threaten either a castle and a king or the queen and the king with her knight. Intent on some plan of his own, Dirk moved his queen out, ready to pounce on a bishop.

"Check," said Elaine, moving her knight.

For once Dirk was astonished, and his surprise and respect pleased her enormously. "Great Scott, the girl can play. Nothing for it but to lose my queen."

Now he played warily and there was no sound except the labored breathing of the patient. Elaine grew tense with the effort to find another weak spot, to surprise Dirk, but he wouldn't be tempted with a spurious offer of her castle. Her queen went down in the capture of a castle and a knight, and each fought to march a pawn across the board to redeem a queen. The best she could do was bring off a stalemate, and considered herself lucky to do that. Dirk was a better player than Bryce, more unorthodox and imaginative, and she failed to anticipate him as she had learned to anticipate Bryce.

"That was a good game," Dirk told her sincerely. "Someone has tutored you well. Another game?"

"No, it's too late." Elaine didn't really want to go. The room was comfortable, with the fire blazing in the fireplace and the wind howling outside. Just as she rose from her chair the lights blinked twice and went out. "What's the matter?"

"Power's off. Sit right there and I'll get a kerosene lamp and a flashlight. Don't worry, they'll have it fixed in an hour or so probably." When Dirk took Elaine's jacket he grumbled, "This is much too light. Here, put my sweater on, it'll do more good than that thing, and I have my leather jacket. Matt, I'm seeing Elaine to the car. Will you be all right?"

The flashlight picked out the steps and Dirk didn't even take her arm in the darkness. That was really sticking to his promise, she thought acidly. Crossing the courtyard with him, she shivered and was grateful for the warm sweater he had given her. The ground was slippery with sleet and she nearly fell, but there was still no helping hand.

"I'd better turn the car for you since I know the driveway."

"No, thank you, I have back-up lights and I can manage." Elaine ducked under his arm to get into the car and pulled out her keys.

"Wait." He went to the other side and slid into the seat next to her. "I just wanted to say—I'm glad you stayed. Would you come out here again? I'd like you to meet Matt when he's himself. He's a wonderful guy."

Matt! "I'll be back to check on him," she said sharply and turned the key in the ignition.

"Don't be like that, Elaine! Can't you at least admit that you enjoyed the evening?"

"I enjoyed the evening," she said coldly. "Are you satisfied? And thank you for an excellent dinner."

Out of the darkness came an unexpected chuckle. "I get it. Now you're angry because I *did* keep hands off. All right, I'll remedy that." His hand shot out to her waist, brought her roughly to his side, and she jerked her head away, gasping with shock. But instead of kissing her he only held her to him until she quieted in his arms. Then gently, carefully, he tipped her face up to his and kissed her.

"This is how it should be," he said softly, and she knew it was true. "I don't want to let you go, I want to keep you with me." His lips brushed the soft brown tendrils of hair on her forehead, moved down across her cheek again to her lips.

CHAPTER EIGHT

Elaine's reaction was rage. Not at first, not while she was driving home, but later when the image of Bryce reasserted itself in her mind. There was rage at herself for forgetting him, guilt for the hurt he would suffer if he ever learned of this evening, this insane lapse into such an emotional state that she lost control of the situation and slipped into a chaotic world. In her normal way of living she did not allow herself to lose her sense of direction, and there was a painful sense of betrayal of Bryce and of herself and her aspirations.

Even greater was her rage at Dirk for being so insistently himself, an intruder into her orderly life, a Pan, who summoned her into the jungle of emotions that she disdained and dreaded. It was hateful of him to recur so vividly in her thoughts and dreams while Bryce faded despite her efforts to fix him in her mind and heart.

When Dirk called her at home the next evening she was ominously restrained. There was no way of avoiding each other at the office, but otherwise she intended not to see him at all and she didn't want to hear from him.

After a silence he said, "I suppose I should have known. It's hard for you to give up a life you know, isn't it? What sort of life could I offer you? No financial security, no prospects of a comfortable home, no outline of a career—I don't know myself what will happen when I finish my graduate work. How can I blame you?"

Whatever she could say after that would sound false and feeble. Instead of feeling virtuous at ending that—episode—she felt subdued and lethargic. It was confusing. She had been prepared for the bitterness, for which she couldn't really blame him, but the resignation, the exoneration, the easy yielding to her didn't fit in with Dirk's character. He wasn't the resigned type.

Well, no matter. She had finished that phase.

She phoned Kitty, who had looked more alarming that morning but insisted on making her calls. One of her roommates answered. Kitty couldn't come to the phone; Molly Carew had brought her home and put her to bed. It was the Asian flu, but not too severe a case. Molly said she'd continue to feel feverish and achy for a while, and would stay in bed and recover completely.

Elaine spent the rest of the evening wirting a long letter to Bryce. Kitty was ill, not seriously, and she herself had spent yesterday with an emergency case; it looked as if an epidemic might be in store. That made it unlikely that she could get home for Thanksgiving, but she hoped to make Christmas a long week end. In Bryce's last letter there had been no mention of his idea of teaching, and to avoid reviving the question she ignored it. She hesitated over mentioning Dirk in connection with the Crawford case, but since Bryce had inquired about Dirk with evident liking, she included a reference to him. She ended with a playful query about Bryce's long silence.

There was a meeting Wednesday morning at which Mrs. Hagstrom explained the plans to combat the epidemic that might strike. The pharmaceutical companies were racing against time to produce quantities of vaccine, especially for medical, teaching, and key civilian personnel. As soon as there was enough on hand, they would begin night clinics, set up in schools and firehouses, and they could expect heavy case loads. Luckily the mortality rate was very low, but the loss in working hours might cripple local industry for a while; and if the epidemic were severe, schools would have to be closed.

It was rather an interesting epidemic, from Elaine's point of view—that is, without being gravely dangerous, it offered good experience squeezed into a short period, and it even seemed exciting in prospect.

For the present her work continued much as usual; the pace did not increase immediately and there was time to attend a couple of county-wide meetings for public health nurses: one on the subject of smoking in relation to lung cancer and heart diseases and another on maturity and the chronically ill patient.

The last interested her greatly; it was so much in line with what Dirk talked about. The lecturing psychiatrist discussed the problem of what makes an invalid of one patient when another, suffering from the same disease and with approximately the same prognosis, recovers partially or completely. He explained it partly in terms of morale, which depended on many factors—attitude of the rest of the family, the home environment, motivation to recover, economic considerations, and so on.

Elaine reported on the meeting at the next staff conference. "The thesis was that at different stages of life we all face different kinds of problems. As babies—surviving, getting enough attention for food, warmth, and care. Later, mastering a language and communication, coping for the first time with social ideas in the nursery schools or playgrounds, learning to think of others, to get along with our families and other children. Then being introduced to formal education, becoming more familiar with the adult world"—she dimpled a little—"discovering the opposite sex, thinking about the place we want to fill in the world. Eventually marriage, work, having and raising children. Lastly, coping with the problems of retirement and aging, feeling out of things, learning to adjust to a new status, which often involves loneliness, leisure, jealousy of younger, active people. The better we do in mastering the problems at each level, the better we're equipped to move on to the next stage and the less likely we are to retrogress when we are confronted with a crisis or difficult situation."

" 'Build thee more stately mansions, O my soul'?" Molly Carew summarized.

"Yes, in a way. As we achieve each new stage with a sense of accomplishment we learn a respect for ourselves and for others that leads to what the lecturer called *intimacy*. Or you might call it self-confidence or faith in our potentials."

Doc leaned forward. "We all have a tendency to retrogress in an illness, to retreat to an earlier stage that has given us more security, like the four-year-old with measles who suddenly demands to be fed and dressed and cuddled as if she were a baby. A few weeks later she'll be independent again if she's basically healthy. Real maturity—at whatever stage—enables us to accept realities and work out our problems in a healthy way."

"That's what the psychiatrist said. But people who haven't really matured are apt to look upon illness as an excuse to dodge other problems and evade issues, so they cling to their illness in order not to face those problems. Some people feel guilty and accept illness as a punishment, and patients like that may become chronic invalids unless we can help restore their vitality, make them want to get better and undertake their responsibilities. Some invalids use their illness to manipulate other people."

As Elaine spoke, it dawned on her that Mrs. Hansom was in the last category and used her illness to dominate the Thompson family. The idea interested her and she wanted to explore it further. But then why did the Thompsons let her dominate the household? Did they feel a sense of guilt about something? It was interesting to speculate about, but Elaine didn't see how the speculations could apply in this case. She saw Dirk give her an approving nod from across the room, but she ignored it. Her only contact with him since the phone call was during short visits to Matt Crawford to check on his progress. Now that Matt was back on his feet, Dirk was in the office more often.

A few days later Elaine was passing Annie Dunne's barn when she saw Katie Serrill's little jalopy parked on the side of the road. On impulse Elaine pulled up too and crossed the road. At her halloo, Katie poked her head out the window in the loft of the barn and waved to her to come up.

Elaine picked her way gingerly past Annie's menagerie of raccoon, squirrel, white mice, and climbed up the ladder into the loft. It was a vast expanse economically lit by the naked light bulb dangling from the center beam. It was so jammed that there was little space for maneuvering, and at first she didn't even see Katie.

"Over here. I'm in the eighteen-thirties. Look for the chalked dates on the floor along the center and you'll see them marked by decades."

Elaine found Katie, thoroughly smudged with dust, going through a Colonial desk. She had stacked the contents in cartons and marked them with slips of paper.

"What a fascinating place," Elaine said, glancing at an open horsehair trunk filled with old costumes, and other odds and ends. She squatted on an ancient battered stool to listen to Katie describe her finds with glowing eyes until she caught some of her friend's enthusiasm.

"It's cold up here," Elaine said finally. "You shouldn't be spending so much time here in this weather."

"All right, boss. Oh, Annie's invited me to have coffee with her. Come and have some too."

Rather agilely for a pregnant girl Katie clambered down the ladder and they started up the path behind the barn to a ramshackle little house that was screened from the road by a stand of elegant tall pines. A wispy-haired, wispy-boned, oldish woman dressed in an ancient housedress with a tattered gray sweater buttoned across her spare chest greeted them at the door.

"Who're you?" she said with a frank inspection of Elaine's face and trim figure. "Nurse? Forrest, Forrest, where'd I hear that name? Eh, Dirk's girl, eh?" The sharp eyes didn't wholly approve.

"Heaven's no," Elaine said emphatically. "Katie must have mentioned me to you."

"Yeah, musta been," said Annie noncommittally. "You good with animals, girl?"

Elaine began to wish she hadn't come. A pair of Siamese cats wound themselves purring around her ankles, and without thinking she bent down to stroke the soft charcoal-colored backs that arched against her. That was password enough for Annie.

"Got some new pets," she announced as they came into the house. She went over to a cage housing a pair of parakeets, lovely little creatures with feathers of blended yellow, chartreuse, and green, and chirped at them, but they wouldn't stir from their perch, only peered with a single eye cocked at her. "Jack and Jill. They're new here and I guess they don't feel at home yet, poor little things. Mrs. Rustad brought 'em over, said she didn't want to bother with 'em and the children wouldn't take care of 'em. Said she knew I'd perk 'em up. That's the way people get you," Annie said wisely with her hands on her hips. "Tell 'em something nice and you can manage 'em." She raked

Elaine with a glance. "Bet that ain't news to you. You get along."

Elaine laughed and discovered that she was beginning to like this woman. No nonsense about her.

"Molly Carew told me you'd had trouble with your arm. How is it these days?" she asked.

"Don't bother me none now. Molly's exercises helped. Good nurse, that girl, but she shoulda married and used it on her family. Well, come and have some coffee."

Something of Annie's tough vitality lingered in Elaine's mind when she went upstairs to see Mrs. Rogers an hour later. It was like seeing Annie projected twenty years into the future, an octogenarian, a woman once as spry and independent as Annie, now bedridden. After giving the bath and hypo she stayed to chat for a few minutes.

Annie, whom Mrs. Rogers knew, was a springboard for her into memories of her life on a farm outside the town some forty, fifty, and sixty years ago. The old woman was full of trenchant comments about the changes in the community and in her life in that time, responding to Elaine's new attitude of sympathy.

"Nice to talk about the old days with someone who's interested," Mrs. Rogers said shyly. "Makes me feel as if I have a new friend."

The pathos of the remark struck Elaine in a delayed reaction. How depressing it must be to be contained within four walls, in a single bed. No wonder she was lonely and reached out for an audience and her memories.

"Don't the children spend much time with you?" Elaine asked, recalling her own visits to her father's parents in the large-roomed house in Evanston, with its turrets and sliding doors and cold pantries and other marvelous attractions.

"Not much. Their mother shoos them outside for fresh air whenever she can; they're kind of peaked." Her eyes softened a little. "A couple times lately the boy's come up and brought some toy animals, and I showed him how our farm looked years ago and told him what his daddy used to do. He wants his daddy to take him out there someday. In the spring maybe, when the forsythia's out or the crocuses are peeping up."

A thought occurred to Elaine, but she was a little uncertain how it would strike Mrs .Rogers. "Have you ever— I mean, did you ever think of wirting down your memories of that farm and how you used to live?"

The old lady snorted. "Me? I ain't no writer. Why should I write about my life? What does that matter—to anyone?" The forlorn sound of her words touched Elaine.

Surprised at her own insistence, she plunged on with her idea. "I know you're no writer, but you'd be surprised how fascinating a plain, matter-of-fact account of a different way of life can be." She told Mrs. Rogers what Katie had been doing with old letters, diaries, records, and about a governess named Hilda Smith who tutored the children of Judge Acheson. "Think how fascinated your grandchildren would be one day to find out how and what you farmed, what kind of meals you served and how they were prepared, the kind of entertainment you enjoyed—husking bees and croquet and square dancing and sleigh riding and all. Did you ever think that you might be able to build a sort of bridge of your memories so that now— and—later your grandchildren will know something about you and your husband and the kind of life you led and what their father did and was like as a child? Don't you think they'd love such real-life stories?"

"But my life was so ordinary." Gramma Rogers was protesting less strenuously. Then, as if afraid of treading on thin ice, she said hesitantly, "You don't think the children would laugh or think it queer of me?" She looked shyly at Elaine for encouragement. "Someday . . . if you truly think they'd like it . . . maybe I'll try it."

"Oh, Mrs. Rogers, do. Just jot down memories at first. You may find they'll make little stories or anecdotes. If you do, I'll type some of them for you, to give you a start." She tore some sheets from her notebook. "Here. Start now. I'll ask your daughter-in-law to bring you some better paper and a pen or pencil. Promise you'll have something ready for me next time?"

Back in the car, Elaine groaned at her impulse. What business was it of hers to intervene in the old lady's life? Didn't she know better than to commit herself to such a chore as typing up chunks of memories in the form of bad grammar and worse spelling? If the old lady actually came up with something . . .

Still she couldn't help smiling over the hopefulness in Mrs. Rogers' faded eyes. Who would have thought the old curmudgeon could be so gentled? In any case, Elaine would call the Senior Citizens' Club to see if any members knew the old lady and could visit her for an hour or two, for a chat or a game of cards.

On the way back to the office she stopped at her post-office box. A note from her father, a letter from a Chicago friend, a bill from the bookstore for a copy of Childe's *What Happened in History?* but still no letter from Bryce. It wasn't like him not to write.

Elaine came in and sat down at her desk to make a call to the Senior Citizens' Club about Mrs. Rogers. When she finished, Kitty was laughing softly behind her.

"What's so funny?"

"Caught in the act! I thought you weren't going to bother with such non-nursing frills as the Senior Citizens' Club."

"Well, ordinarily I wouldn't, but in this case——" Kitty's giggle was too infectious and Elaine had to smile at herself too.

"All right, so I turned over a new leaf. I was wrong. Period. I'm beginning to see that it's pretty hard to separate the physical and emotional well-being in some of these cases, but that doesn't mean I'm a complete convert. But I should have my head examined." She told Kitty about the encounter with Katie and Annie Dunne and the subsequent call on Mrs. Rogers and the torrent of memories that had been unleashed. "I must be getting softheaded to volunteer to type up a bunch of scribbled notes. Sudden interest in local history, heaven knows why, unless I caught it from Katie today."

"Hmmm. Elaine, I almost suspect you of beginning to like our Kahopac."

"Oh, shush, can't you see I'm busy?" She turned to concentrate on her reports.

After a moment Kitty said sympathetically, "Nothing from Bryce again today?"

Elaine shook her head.

"He's probably terribly busy, especially if he's begun teaching," Kitty offered as explanation.

"Oh, I don't think it's on his mind any more," Elaine said. "He hasn't mentioned it since he was here. Anyhow it wouldn't be like him to take a teaching job without at least letting me know. But his silence worries me. Maybe I'll phone him tonight and see how things are."

"You'll probably find he's just been jammed with work. Didn't he say there's some big hush-hush project under way this month?" Kitty suddenly clapped hand to her forehead. "Sievehead that I am, I nearly forgot. Dirk came upstairs an hour ago to find out whether you would drive him out to the Thompsons. He's anxious to start on their case history or something. He's working downstairs in the conference room in case you can make it this afternoon. It's not too late, is it?"

"Oh!" Elaine jerked a sheet of paper out of her typewriter,

crumpled it, and threw it into her wastebasket. "No, I suppose it's not too late." She didn't look forward to an encounter with him, but it would happen sooner or later and she might as well underscore her intention to keep their relations impersonal. "All right."

She needn't have worried. Dirk was perfectly impersonal during the drive and their call on the Thompsons. He took no notes during the visit but afterward asked if she could stop for a minute along the road so he could jot down some notes. He asked a few businesslike questions and scribbled down her answers, which were terse and matter-of-fact.

"Are you always so businesslike in your calls as you were to-day?" he asked, still scribbling.

"Well, I don't waste a lot of time after I've accomplished what I came for, if that's what you mean," she said. "I don't consider it fair to my other patients to linger when the work is done. And I remember our professors warned us against getting too personally involved with our patients." A little guiltily she thought of her call on Mrs. Rogers today. She glanced restlessly at her watch.

"It's possible to be sympathetic without getting involved," Dirk said mildly, still writing.

Finally he closed his notebook and stuck it in his breast pocket. "Thanks. Hope this hasn't delayed you too long, but I wanted to get as much down as possible. . . . My aunt took quite a liking to you today," he added with no change in tone. "She said you were very much interested in her treasures in the barn."

"It was fascinating. I'd like to go back again with Katie some time—after work."

"Annie would be delighted. If you don't mind, I'd like to visit the Thompsons again, but now that I know them I think it will be proper to come alone; you needn't be troubled to take me."

She ignored the last part of his comment. "Yes, they understand that you're making a study with our cooperation. I hope you don't run into trouble with Mr. Thompson."

"You don't have much use for him, do you?"

Elaine shrugged. "What little I've seen of him doesn't exactly add to my respect for him, when I consider what straits the family is in and how hard his wife works to run the house and take care of her mother and the family."

"I might have guessed where your sympathies would lie," said Dirk drily. "It struck me that just possibly the wife was acting the martyr and escaping some of her own responsibilities to her husband and child by her preoccupation with her mother. And why such a preoccupation to the exclusion of husband and child? Have you tried to find out much of the story behind all this?"

"Why should I?" Elaine retorted. "I'm there to give medical treatment, not to psychoanalyze them."

"Umm. Molly Carew gives her patients medical treatment too, but one reason she's such a valuable nurse is that she uses her full intelligence and intuition and human sympathies as well. I get the impression that you think you can split the human element and the medical aspects of the case."

"Obviously you disagree," Elaine said sharply. She was tempted to absolve herself by speaking of what she had learned in her visit to Mrs. Rogers, but she refused to give him the satisfaction of defending herself. Let him think whatever he wanted; it was of no concern to her. "I'll be interested in seeing what kind of solution you might suggest for the Thompsons," she said with abrupt challenge.

"It looks pretty hopeless, doesn't it?" he said mildly. "That's no easy job. Have you talked it over with Frieda? She might have some good suggestions."

That touched a sore spot with Elaine. She was more inclined to follow her own way and steer clear of Frieda's counsel than Kitty, for instance. It was partly her independence, partly a reluctance to accept counsel in matters that she considered primarily a nurse's concern, though she had come to value Phil Roland's contributions in physical therapy—they were a little more tangible and she was readier to admit their relevance.

"Not yet," she said evasively. She released the brake and steered the car back on the road.

"By the way, how is Bryce?" Dirk's tone was carefully impersonal and Elaine couldn't legitimately object to the question.

"Fine." Since that was both unnecessarily terse and not quite true, she added honestly, "I haven't heard from him for a while, but I assume he is." She promised herself to make that call as soon as she reached home that evening.

CHAPTER NINE

It was anything but a satisfactory telephone conversation. Bryce seemed abstracted, and Elaine had the feeling that it was a bad connection in every way. His voice sounded remote and unreachable. It was only at the beginning when he seemed surprised and pleased at her unexpected call that she had a sense of pleasure and intimacy, but almost immediately a barrier rose between them when she tentatively asked why he hadn't written.

"It's because—well, I was just writing to you about it. I'll let the letter speak for me. How are Kitty and Dirk and the Serrills?"

They chatted for a while and then she hung up, disturbed by his tone and evasive manner.

The letter reached her two days later and turned her world topsy-turvy. She read it through hurriedly and came back to study the key paragraphs. It seemed so unlike Bryce that it was hard for her to grasp.

"It was too good an opportunity to miss, Elaine. It's a school that I'm familiar with; I know the principal is liberal in his policies and eager to build up a fine teaching staff, and I won't have to coach a football or basketball team along with my other duties. If I hadn't taken the job it would have meant waiting another year, and I was anxious to get started.

"I fully intended to tell you right away, but I was so busy the time slipped by without my notice. I know, Elaine dear, that you will be distressed about not being consulted and I'm deeply sorry, but it was a decision I had to make.

"I can't help, lately, feeling that we are pulling in different directions, and it makes me very unhappy. It seems to me that you have built up a picture of me in your mind with an aura of importance that I simply don't have. At the same time I have an uneasy awareness that you dismiss things quite airily that often have great importance for me.

"You know that I'm devoted to you and have looked forward eagerly—more so than you, I think—to our marriage and still do. My darling, it's terribly hard to say this, but if you are dissatisfied with the course my life seems to be taking, if you cannot picture yourself fitting into it, I can only say that you should put your happiness before loyalty to me and our pledges to each other.

"If you should decide to marry me anyhow, it will make me very happy, but I dread any concession to convention, any glossing over of deep feelings, any semblance of dishonesty or false pretensions. I want very much to teach; I want you to share my life; but I do not want you to abandon your own hopes if they conflict with mine.

"Whatever you decide, you will always be dear to me and I hope we shall never lose our friendship.

"All my love,
"Bryce."

It was impossible. Elaine simply could not reconcile this firm Bryce with the one she knew, so amenable to reason, so deferent to her wishes. Why, this fantastic Bryce even set a career before his marriage to her! It was beyond belief.

She thrust the letter, folded, into her purse and drove to the office as usual, with every semblance of her professional manner. She made out records and call slips, made her calls, changed bandages, gave injections, counseled a young mother on feeding her baby, called two doctors to discuss a change of prescription, made a visit to an orthopedic clinic with a deformed child, and returned to the office that afternoon without the slightest memory of how the day had passed. Only the scribbled notes she had automatically made after each call enabled her to summon some dim memories for the purposes of her records.

When everyone had left the office she slowly put her desk in order and thought hazily that there was some ordeal ahead. What was it? She took out a compact to powder her face and saw the letter. This time the mere sight of Bryce's writing seared. Her hand trembled when she lifted the letter from her purse. She stared at it with the anguish that she had held at bay all day long, and the phrases reshaped themselves before her eyes.

"Pulling in different directions . . . a picture of me with an aura of importance . . . cannot picture yourself fitting into it . . . dread any glossing over . . . any semblance of dishonesty . . . whatever you decide . . ."

She could not bring herself to touch it again although she stretched out her hand to restore the letter to her purse. She snapped it shut, switched out the lights, and stumbled blindly out of the room, down the stairway and into her car. With her hand on the wheel she regained a sense of familiarity and drove out of the yard in a downpour of rain.

It simply could not be so. She must have misread the letter, misinterpreted it, and tomorrow morning she would come back to find that it was something else entirely, that Bryce had *not* taken that job, that things were as they always had been, that he was pressing her to marry him. She clearly remembered that it ended, "All my love," as it always had. *Ergo*, Bryce still loved her.

The windshield blurred more and more in the rain even though the wipers spun at top speed back and forth, back and forth. It hypnotized her . . . more rain, raindrops, harsh tears beating against the glass, splashing, shimmering in the dizzying lights of oncoming cars, blinding her one after another.

Around the curve of the highway flashed another set of lights straight into her eyes. There was a shriek of brakes; she twisted the wheel away from the other car and skidded at a tilt onto the wet shoulder.

Elaine collapsed over the wheel in a torrent of tears. Under her shaking arms the horn blasted in spasms of sound. Abruptly the car door was yanked open, the rain poured in, and someone slid into the seat beside her.

"Elaine! Are you all right? Oh, thank God." Hands seized her by the shoulders and raised her back against the seat.

"She all right, Dirk?" said another looming figure, opening the door. "Lord, I thought she'd tear straight into that last one."

"She's very upset but I don't think she's been hurt. She's been crying, must have been blinded by tears. Phil, I'll take her home, you go on."

"Okay, if you're sure she's all right. See you tomorrow."

The door slammed but Elaine couldn't stop weeping. Dirk gathered her to him, his hand pressed her head against his shoulder, and his voice soothed her. Gradually her tears diminished and she became dimly aware that Dirk was shaking. Her sobs ceased at last and she rested against his wet coat without speaking, without thinking.

Finally she drew a long breath and said out of a haze, "Dirk? Where did you come from? What happened?"

His hand cradled her face. "Feeling better now? Good heavens, I thought you would smash right into that car that came around the bend." His voice lost some of its tautness and he went on more calmly. "When you came downstairs Phil and I were in the conference room talking over a case. You passed by without a word when we called to you and you looked so strange that we got worried so we piled into Phil's car and followed you. We had a hard time catching up, you were driving so fast, and when that last car tore around that curve we thought sure . . . Anyhow you're all right now." Abruptly he released her. "Move over, I'll drive you home."

As he started the car he grew suddenly angry. "What do you mean by driving when you're in such a state anyhow? And in this deluge! You might have been . . . Are you crazy?"

"What state?" Elaine said meekly.

"How do I know. For heavens' sake, don't ever drive like that when something has happened to upset you!" Emptied of belligerence, he slowed down himself, peering through the rain that was turning into snow. After a minute he said, "What was it, Elaine? What upset you?"

Unwillingly she said, "A letter," and wondered why she troubled to answer at all.

"Oh." There was a brief pause. "From Bryce, of course." Acid came into his voice. "So he's going into teaching after all, and you don't like it. Was that all?"

She didn't like the iciness that wiped out the solicitude, and said in a subdued tone, "Not that. He . . . we're not getting married."

She breathed quickly to stave off another outburst of tears. Dirk might disapprove of her, but she wanted him to know the facts—so he'd disapprove of her for the right reasons, she thought with a miserable effort at humor. He ought to be satisfied; Bryce had asserted himself, as Dirk had foreseen, rebelling against her managing of their lives. Well, there it was, she told herself, now face it. Bryce's revolt had shown that they had different goals, different ideals, different values. Her vision of herself was shrinking to pitiful proportions, squeezing her self-esteem into a tiny ball. But that ball still held enough ego and pride to make her clutch at any hope.

Maybe it wasn't what Dirk had forecast. Maybe Bryce had met another girl who was influencing him. Perhaps if she went back now to Chicago before it was too late, she could patch things up, make them right again. That must be it, it couldn't be anything as abstract as a principle. There had to be another girl involved or Bryce would not feel her own lacks so keenly.

Unconsciously she sat up straighter, forgetting she was not alone. "That's it," she whispered to herself. "If I go back and talk with him . . . It must be another girl . . ."

"Stop kidding yourself!" Harshly Dirk's words cut into her train of thought. "Face the facts, Elaine!" The car swept violently around the curve up the hill.

"Watch out!" Alarm restored her to the present. "If you can't drive better than that let me take over again," she snapped. When he shot a savage look at her, she lapsed into silence while he drove up the hill to the Flandrau house. It was snowing now, big, wet flakes. Dirk parked the car in the garage and turned off the ignition. Neither stirred.

"I'm sorry I yelled at you like that, but you gave me such a scare."

"I wasn't driving when you yelled at me this time," she pointed out coldly.

"I know, but you're so exasperating! Whenever I think you're on the verge of facing something and licking it . . ." He made an effort to control himself, and spoke more gently. "Truly, Elaine, I'm sorry you have to undergo an experience like this. Being jilted——"

Trust him to find the brutal phrase, Elaine thought resentfully.

"Being jilted is tough, even if you phrase it graciously as I'm sure Bryce would. It's happened to me and I know how it can smash your ego and all those handsome pictures you build up of yourself and the kind of life you want to lead. Your self-respect can be at low ebb for a long time, but in this case I think it's your pride that's taking the worst beating. It often is. That's natural. It hurts to think either that you've chosen badly or that this very special person with whom you identify yourself for some unaccountable reason doesn't choose you. I suspect it's harder on you than on most people because you're more used to having things go the way you want."

"You don't have to sympathize with me, thanks!"

"Elaine, I don't know how to say this properly—maybe it can't be acceptable however it's put, but I must say it and I hope you'll hear me out. Remember the first time I saw you, on the train? I thought what a very pretty girl you were, how smooth, how untouched somehow, and I couldn't help speculating whether you were a cold fish, to put it bluntly——"

"Thank you."

"Or whether you might become quite wonderful, quite human, under emotional fire of some kind, in some sort of ordeal. I would have guessed you to be a model or debutante . . ."

"I remember you said that."

". . . and sized you up as a self-centered egotist. But when it turned out that you are a nurse, it didn't seem to fit the pattern, and that intrigued me. It's not the kind of work an egotist is likely to choose. When I knew you better, I wondered whether perhaps Bryce had influenced you, and then Kitty told me more, about your background and your father's illness and your mother, and the picture began to make more sense."

"That must be very gratifying." She could not refrain from sarcasm. "But I don't see the need for all this analysis. I shall manage quite well." Yet she made no move to leave. It was a new experience to undergo this kind of critical personal evaluation; no one had ever talked to her so bluntly before. She had the same urge to qualify well that made her rate high in nurse's training, in her classes in biology and chemistry, in anatomy and physiology. Even with Dirk she wanted to qualify. Especially with Dirk, she admitted to herself.

"I resent the way you maneuver people and I've got to say that I'm glad Bryce finally revolted. I keep telling myself I'm crazy to get tangled up with a girl like you. I admire your ability, your intelligence, your purposefulness, but I can't stand those blind spots—the impersonal way you deal with your patients, your impatience with the element of sympathy that makes a real woman. Every time I think you're coming out of that shell, I begin thinking about the kind of woman you might be. Tonight when I saw you break up emotionally I believed that the warmth was there under the ice and control or you wouldn't react so strongly."

"Well, this is a most astonishing lecture! What am I supposed to make of it?" she fired at him, blazing with anger at his forthrightness.

"Elaine, I thought being honest with you . . . Never mind! I apologize for the lecture. I *was* crazy to think of you!" He got out of the car, slammed the door shut, and stalked off into the snow.

Elaine jumped out of the car and ran to the garage door. "Dirk, don't go like that! Dirk, wait! You can't go in this snow. Come back, I'll call a cab!"

Already the snow had curtained him and down the road she could barely hear the quick crunching of his feet on snow. What a stubborn man! She ran back to start the car, backed it out; abruptly it sputtered and died. She had forgotten to stop for gas!

"Blast it!" She sat still, listening, but there was no sound of returning steps.

119

She ran into the house and upstairs without a word to Cora.

Half an hour later came a discreet tap on the door. "Have you had dinner, Miss Forrest? I saved something for you if you want it."

Elaine sat up on the bed. She hadn't eaten, but she didn't want anything. "Oh, thank you, Cora, not tonight." The bedspread was damp from her wet coat and she shook it off while Cora's footsteps sounded softly down the carpeted hallway.

She hung it in her bathroom to dry, and lay back on her bed again without switching on the lights. Talk about emotional barriers—if Dirk only knew how emotions were whirling around in her until she ached from the strain. It was a merry-go-round of emotions; at one moment grief over Bryce; at the next, anger at Dirk, at herself, bewilderment at not knowing her own mind, at finding herself for the first time uncertain which way to turn. And somewhere, sandwiched between all these, a glimmering of understanding and unwonted humility.

The ordeal was here all right, and it was like a touchstone. Touch it here and she'd return to the safe life she had always known; even now, she thought, if she went back to Chicago she could mend things with Bryce, on her own terms if she chose, she thought with a flare of pride. But the flare flickered out. She discovered that she did not honestly want that. She didn't want Bryce to capitulate to her now; she wanted him to be a man. For the first time she understood that she had no real desire to marry a man who could not choose his own course, make his own decisions, be what he wanted to be.

Then suppose she accepted Bryce on his own terms and became the wife of a high school teacher. She began to smile at herself in the dark. Was that so terrible after all? She toyed distastefully with visions of herself being chummy with teachers and their wives, playing chaperone to adolescents, coping with heaven knew what sort of problems. If only Bryce would take a college job, she thought wryly. That did it. Inexorably she led herself to the next step—face it, Elaine, you're a snob. It's the social status that bothers you; you wouldn't mind if he were a college professor. And it wasn't as if she hadn't known many teachers who were stimulating, interesting, and enlivening. It was sheer snobbery.

Triumphantly she sat up. If that's the worst, you can go through with it, she told herself. She would write Bryce now and tell him she had been plain snobbish about it, and now that she understood that fact and the importance of teaching to him, she had changed her mind and wanted to marry him still. That was it!

She switched on the light over her desk, took out the typewriter, inserted paper, and began typing.

"Dearest Bryce:

"Now that you have made me understand the importance of your work to you, which I should have known long ago, I want to . . ."

It was cleansing to get it down on paper and yet her fingers faltered over the keys and stopped. She began once more and again tore out the paper. She crumpled up four sheets before she could take the next step.

She faced the realization that she did not want to marry Bryce any more, and the cause of the change had nothing to do with his decision to teach. She was fond of him, devoted to him, loved him—but she did not want to marry him.

At first she refused to face the reason for the change, but it asserted itself in spite of her. She traced it back to that night at Leo's when she danced with Dirk. She told herself she wasn't in love with Dirk, but that brief experience revealed how easy it would be to succumb . . . She stopped phrasing it in her mind, but not before she had sensed the contrast between her placid feeling for Bryce and the tempestuous emotion that Dirk could arouse in her.

One thing she was sure of, and Dirk's words bore out the truth of it. There was too wide a gulf between her and Dirk to permit any deep relationship to develop, and moreover . . .

And moreover, she thought bitterly, she had given him little cause to think well of her. Her cheeks burned at the recollection of her arrogance and thoughtlessness.

Most of the night she lay awake in a state of depression and new humility tangled with bewilderment that the things she had been so sure of, her plans and hopes for marriage, Bryce, her very self, should be so baseless and insecure. How could this happen to her?

Early in the morning, unable to sleep, she took a shower, dressed, and sat down again at the typewriter. She had learned that the touchstone could not restore the security and life she had known. The best it could do was to invoke a new area, a new stage of life and she had no idea what that would include. Not Bryce, not Dirk, but her work, her friends, her father—and someone unknown. But she was discovering new qualities in herself, new strengths as well as perplexities.

Now she was ready to write Bryce honestly about the turmoil she was experiencing and the things she was trying to learn. She ended with:

"If this causes you pain, I am sorry. It hurts me to uncover these things about myself too. I think perhaps in saying no, we must not marry, I am learning how close is the relationship between us, how deeply rooted in these past few years, and not least of all how much you have taught me with your kindness and your integrity. There is a void within, of course, and must be for you too. So much has been uprooted for me in this single day and night. It seems strange that it is less than 24 hours since I read your letter. All my love,

                                    "Elaine."

She put on a coat and went downstairs to the terrace. The early sun was breaking up rosy clouds in the east and the smell of rain was strong and fresh; a damp wind ruffled Elaine's hair. She walked down to the little summerhouse and sat watching the sunrise. She started when a wet nose pushed itself against her leg. It was the big collie from the Serrill house, his coat thick, warm and comforting against her leg. He laid his head on her knees and the brown mournful, intelligent eyes gazed at her. She stroked him gently as she sat there, lost in thought.

The milkman's truck rattling up the Flandrau driveway restored her sense of time and reminded her that she was out of gas. She hailed the milkman and he generously siphoned enough gas from his own tank to enable her to get safely down the mountain to the nearest gas station.

Perhaps you learn most in solitude and pain, Elaine mused; you come closer to yourself and the bare bones of reality. This was the worst she had been through since her father almost died. Perhaps worse. Then she had been a frightened schoolgirl and it was sad and terrible to face the loss of a father, but could it be worse than trying to face yourself? Wasn't that the hardest thing of all? In time you could adjust to anything else, but if you didn't come to grips with yourself, nothing could ever come out right.

The loneliness was overlaid with a sense of having met a crisis and mastered it, but she was still tilting with her new insecurity and uncertainty.

Elaine worked soberly through the day and was surprised that it wasn't joyless. The sun brought back a whisper of fall, and a few leaves still clung to the steadfast oaks.

She couldn't bring herself to tell Kitty about Bryce's letter; the wound was too fresh and tender. Dirk stayed away from the office that day. Elaine made her final visit to Matt Crawford to make sure there had been no relapses, and stayed to talk a little with him. Dirk wasn't mentioned but he hovered in the background when Matt talked about his painting and books and music. He was amused at her surprise at his familiarity with the Art Institute of Chicago—he could refer feelingly to the Chagall Rabbi, to the huge "Sunday on the Grande Jatte" of Seurat, to a small Picasso—as well as with the New York museums, but he made no concession to her thinly veiled curiosity.

"Just accept the fact that people don't always stay in categories," he said cryptically as she left.

There were several visits to patients with the Asian flu; the epidemic was beginning to sweep through the county and more than one school had already closed down. What a time for an epidemic, just before Christmas. With her usual foresight Elaine had spent the previous week end in New York, shopping for her Kahopac and Chicago friends, and had been particularly delighted to find for Bryce exactly the kind of V-necked Cashmere sweater she had been looking for. It had been packed and sent home with the other presents so that she could travel light on her brief trip home.

At the office that afternoon Mrs. Hagstrom came upstairs to make assignments for the flu clinics now that the vaccine shipments had been received.

"As you know, this means we'll be working overtime a good deal, but I hope you will all be very careful to get enough rest and food; we can't spare you at a time like this." She smiled a little. "It's hard on the younger members of our staff, but perhaps they can ease up a bit on social life for a couple of weeks when the epidemic is at its worst." She relapsed into a graver mood. "We don't anticipate any serious cases, but we must remember that although most people recover readily, there have been a very few mortalities, and we must be on guard to spot any cases that should have hospital care.

"And one other thing, which I bring up most reluctantly.

You know our policy of keeping one person on duty through the holidays. Miss Schwartz and Molly have both volunteered for Christmas Day, but if the epidemic continues until Christmas, Kitty and Elaine, would you two be able to stay on duty if it seems necessary? It's a shame we're so shorthanded, but there have been unexpected delays for the two nurses who were supposed to begin working here in December. Luckily, we have the help of two former members of the staff who are now housewives and mothers, but of course their contribution has to be limited."

Kitty said at once that she would be available and Elaine, with some reluctance, said she would be glad to remain. But she did not relish the thought of missing Christmas at home, even though without Bryce it would be very different from the Christmas she had anticipated. What a dismal ending to her year these last few days had wrought.

CHAPTER TEN

Only four of Elaine's patients were hospitalized. Doc had hesitated about one of them, a college girl, but he finally sent her to the county hospital.

It was the day before Christmas when Elaine finally gave up and phoned her father that she couldn't get away. He was even more upset than she thought he would be; he always seemed so self-sufficient and phlegmatic that she never realized how very much he really missed her and how disappointed he was now that their Christmas would be spoiled. He had taken it for granted, of course, that Bryce would share it with them, and she was a little relieved that she didn't yet have to break that news to her father.

Yesterday's clinic had had to be canceled, so on Christmas Eve, Elaine and Kitty helped Doc handle the double attend-ance. At the firehouse they covered the pool table with a clean white cloth, laid out a basin, tray with clean towels, syringes and needles, alcohol, mounds of white cotton balls, and the small yellow and white boxes with the influenza vaccine. Elaine gloomily predicted that no one would show up on Christmas Eve anyhow.

When the doctor appeared, flushed and apologetic about his delay—his car had been stuck in a snowdrift after his last call—the men lined up and rolled up their sleeves. The girls swabbed their arms with alcohol, prepared the needles for the assembly operation, and joked with the men who were squeamish and couldn't bear to watch the injections.

After the first hour each man had become nothing to Elaine but a shirt or jacket with a sleeve to be rolled up, a muscular arm to be punctured—sweatered, shirted, vested in plaid, red flannel, wool, corduroy, brown suede—each with a differing aura of cigarette smoke, gum, beer, cigar, pipe tobacco, hair lotion, shaving lotion, even a lingering perfume. When the last sleeve was rolled down, Kitty propelled Doc over to an arm-chair in the recreation room of the firehouse. "You need rest, Doctor. Let me prescribe half an hour of relaxation over a beer and a TV program."

The fire chief gallantly brought Cokes for the girls and of-fered cookies from a secret store in the kitchen. Two or three firemen, a school principal, the school janitor, and the town clerk sat around with them, chatting with a pleasantly let-down feeling after the rush of organizing and working.

Elaine sat with her feet propped up on a chair, quietly sip-ping her Coke, amusedly viewing Kitty describing a session with an unmanageable patient for the benefit of the men. Someone turned on the TV and Elaine leaned back in her chair and half drowsed through the program of Christmas hymns. The year before, she and her father and Bryce had attended Christmas Eve services in church.

An odd sort of contentment seeped through her lethargy and it occurred to her that she had come to love this work. For all the grousing she did, there was enormous variety and satisfac-tion in it. Whether it was helping to care for a boy with mul-tiple sclerosis or to restore a cardiac patient to health and activity—or whether it was merely persuading a superstitious, doting grandmother that the two-year-old granddaughter in her care would not catch pneumonia if she lowered the house tem-perature from 80 to 72—it was rewarding.

It had been a difficult time for her personally, and yet she woke each day eager to see her old patients and care for the new ones. The paper work was a nuisance and yet essential; she remembered her annoyance more than once in the omission of vital data so that she had to waste time repeating interviews and irritating some patients at the duplication of information.

There was something else too. It struck Elaine that once she would have ignored men like these, so different in personality and type, so remote from her previous experience of people; and in doing so would have missed the richness of range that she now valued. Once she might have resented Kitty's being in the limelight; now it troubled her not at all. A deep fondness had developed between them, as if Kitty were the kind of sister Elaine had always wanted. Also, Elaine was aware that she didn't have to perform for these men to win their liking. She sensed that they had a feeling for her and Kitty that was compounded of respect, liking, and a certainty that if there was trouble, they could be counted on.

Afterward she and Kitty would spend an hour or two with the Serrills, so it would end as a pleasant Christmas Eve after all. And tomorrow she would spend with Doc and Connie, after exchanging presents with Mrs. Flandrau and Cora.

A call from the hospital summoned Doc to the phone. He came back with a grave, tired face. At first he was evasive of their queries but finally confessed it was about the young college girl in the hospital, whom he had visited that afternoon. She had seemed to be improving, but an hour ago she had died.

"Oh, no!" Elaine was shocked. The girl had kindled her interest and she had specially asked Doc about her and been happy at the indications of a recovery.

"I think it's the first death in the county," he said in grim, quiet tones, against a background of "Adeste Fidelis" on T.V. Someone turned the set off and the room was quiet. Doc picked up his coat and shouldered into it like an old man. "I hope there will be no others. Merry Christmas," he said gruffly, and the door closed behind him.

"I can't get over it," Elaine said softly, and Kitty touched her shoulder in sympathy. "Her poor family."

Silently the girls put on their coats and gathered their bags, said good-by to the now subdued men, and went down to Kitty's car. The night crackled with the cold and they were grateful for the heater's warmth.

"Kitty," Elaine said presently, "I've been wanting to tell you, but I couldn't until now. Bryce and I have broken our engagement."

The car skidded slightly on ice and lurched forward again as Kitty shot her friend an astonished look. "Oh, Elaine, no! I knew something was wrong, but I had no idea it could be that! Why, Elaine? Why?"

When Elaine finished telling her the bare outline, Kitty broke out again, "But are you sure it's final? Won't you reconsider? Haven't you missed him terribly?"

"Not so terribly," Elaine answered slowly. "Not as much as I thought I would. Partly because we've been so swamped with work, but besides that—well, what I thought was love was more like a devoted friendship and—a little bit—a misleading feeling that our marriage would be so—so *appropriate*. Bryce is so much the kind of person I thought I wanted to marry."

There was a long pause. "Does Dirk have something to do with this change?" Kitty asked.

"No, of course not!" Elaine said violently.

"Well, maybe it sounds silly to you, but I've a notion that he's more than casually interested in you. Something about the way he watches you——"

"It does sound silly," said Elaine abruptly and looked out the window. "He spends his time thinking up nasty things about me. He thinks I'm cold and self-centered and everything that's disagreeable, and don't think he hasn't told me so. And he's smug and arrogant and stubborn and . . . well, anyhow, no!"

"I don't think he is at all like that," Kitty protested, "and I've never heard him say a word of criticism. I think you're crazy, making him out to be some sort of ogre."

"Let's not talk about it! Would you stop at my place for a minute so I can pick up some gifts, and then we'll go back down the hill?"

Katie was noticeably bulging and more awkward these days, but her greeting was as lively as ever. She looked very pretty in an embroidered mandarin-collared maternity jacket and skirt of dark satin, and she and Paul proudly showed off their eight-foot Christmas tree.

"I was afraid you'd be delayed longer so I planned a late supper," she said happily. "Oh, that must be Dirk now. Paul, will you . . . ? I'm not as springy as I used to be."

Laughing over some private joke with Paul, Dirk came in, not at all disconcerted to see the girls, with a few packages to put under the tree. It was awkward but Elaine didn't want to spoil the evening, so she smiled and even offered her hand to demonstrate how very hail-fellow, well-met she intended to be. Kitty gave her a speculative glance.

There was a pleasant supper, with Katie and Paul joking about the baby who would enjoy the next Christmas with them, and then opening the presents in the warmth of the blazing fire, with even a creaking rubber bone for the collie. One present for Elaine was beautifully wrapped with a card that read mysteriously, *"For my daughter with Katie's help."*

Completely puzzled, Elaine unwrapped the package, found a golden box and lifted off the cover to find a dusty, moldering old album. If she hadn't known Katie so well, she would have suspected a practical joke, but she looked at her in consternation.

"Go on," Katie urged with barely contained excitement. "Open it."

"It doesn't look exactly appetizing," Elaine said dubiously. She touched the album gingerly and dust came off on her fingers. "What does the card mean? Where did you find . . . ? Oh! Something from Annie's barn? What in the world is it? I can hardly read the printing, it's so faded. L-O-G-A-N—The Logan Family Album! Oh, Katie, you darling."

Eagerly she began to thumb through it and her face fell. "But hardly any of the pictures are identified. How would I know which of these faces belongs to my mother?"

"There must be some way of identifying them," Paul said. "There are some papers underneath that might give some clues. Katie's been dying to inspect them, but she swore she'd save them for you."

Elaine sent Katie an appreciative smile. "Here's a bundle of letters. There seem to be documents of some kind—birth certificates, insurance policies, diplomas—oh, here's a family Bible —driver's licenses, playbills, goodness knows what all."

"You'd be surprised how interesting and full of information they can be when you put them into some sort of order," Katie said. "Paul and I have worked over several batches of material and we generally manage to extract quite a lot of interesting stuff."

It became a sort of detective game, a challenge, and the rest of Christmas Eve was spent in a joint effort to ferret out clues to enable them to identify the pictures. The old family Bible with its yellowed pages dated back to the eighteenth century and the first entry read: *"Given to my son Thomas Jonathan Logan on the day of his departure from Hingham, England, to a new country across the seas, March 18, 1747."* Three years later was entered Thomas' marriage to Hannah Livingston and in the next year the first American-born Logan. There was also an entry for Elaine's mother: *"Phyllis Logan, b. April 10, 1910, d. Jonathan Jay Logan and Priscilla Fletcher."*

Katie had even found a daguerreotype of Elaine's grandmother Priscilla in her late teens. Thoroughly intrigued, Elaine could hardly wait to examine everything in her prize package.

"There may be something more in the trunk I was going through," Katie volunteered, "but I haven't had time to finish. Remember the horsehair trunk next to the desk I was working on when you came in that day? That's the one."

"Oh, I've got to go back one day and see if there's more," Elaine exclaimed.

It was late and time to leave when they discovered it had been snowing and the ground was covered with two inches of snow. Elaine refused Kitty's offer of a ride home; she wanted to walk home in the snow; it was only a half-mile walk or so.

"Then I'll walk you home," Dirk said, "and I'll pick up my car later. All right, Paul?"

Remembering her last encounter with Dirk, Elaine was not enthusiastic but could not gracefully refuse his company. First he stopped at his car and picked up a package, which he carried under his arm without comment, and then they went on up the hill toward the Flandrau house with the flakes falling on their backs and the wind whipping Elaine's coat around her. It was quiet in the night and nothing much was said until they reached the shelter of the courtyard where it was easier to talk.

"You seemed rather quiet tonight at first," Dirk remarked.

"We were tired, we just came from a flu clinic."

"Kitty didn't seem so tired. But I suppose it's upsetting to be away from home when you'd counted on a vacation and seeing your father again—and maybe Bryce."

"Yes," Elaine said after a pause. "But the thing that really hit me was that a patient of mine died tonight." Her eyes filled with tears; the irony of her finding a mother on Christmas Eve and the loss of some mother's daughter had been on her mind most of the evening. She turned her head away from the light and cleared her throat. "Well, good night Dirk, and thank you for walking me home. Merry Christmas." Suddenly remembering that Dirk was an orphan, she said on impulse, "Where do you usually spend your Christmas?"

He shrugged. "With friends who are footloose sometimes. Tomorrow with my aunt and Matthew Crawford. The three little Rustad boys always come to visit Annie in the afternoon and we'll open a few presents." But that wasn't on his mind, and he added quietly, "That must have been the college girl who died of Asian flu? It was reported on the radio as I was driving over. I'm awfully sorry, Elaine. One of those inexplicable things."

He opened the door for her and they stood in the hallway for a silent moment. Then she politely asked if he'd like to have a cup of coffee, and with equal politeness he declined, wished her a Merry Christmas, and left. When she opened the closet door to hang up her coat she noticed that he had left his package on the hall table. She picked it up, ready to call him back, when she saw it was addressed to her.

"Merry Christmas, Elaine. This is something Matt gave me years ago which I'd like you to have—in memorium, I suppose."

She unwrapped it and found a beautifully carved Indian chess set. Her reaction was mixed—relief at this indication of Dirk's acceptance of a truce that superseded the tension between them, and perplexity. He had evidently known that she would be at the Serrills' and yet he had left the package in the car. Did that mean he wasn't sure he wanted to give it to her? If he hadn't been sure, why not? Had it depended on her attitude or actions? Had he been disappointed in her?

But looking at the set, picking up the queen, she thought he couldn't have been too disappointed in her or he surely wouldn't have wanted to yield something that must have been a treasure to him, both for its intrinsic value and for its association with Matt. One didn't give away a set like that on a whim.

Dawn brought a sparkling Christmas morning, with just enough snow on the ground to make for caution in driving and to decorate the landscape with a fringe of white on trees and bushes and a carpet on the ground.

Elaine drove to the office, deciding to call her father in the afternoon. It would be a lonely Christmas for him unless he spent it at the club, and the holiday was certainly not a clubable one. There were his friends, of course, but no one really close since Doc's departure.

"Whew, I think we can begin to relax a little next week," Molly Carew said, going over her records. "Fewer cases last week for everyone so far, and I think we're past the peak. Maybe we'll even get New Year's Day off, who knows?"

Kitty and Miss Schwartz would relieve them in the afternoon. No one on Elaine's list of calls seemed seriously ill. For her last call she drove up a bumpy dirt road to an outlying district, scrambled over the ridge of the wooded hill, and skidded to a stop in front of the most decrepit of the little shacks that huddled in the clearing on the hill.

In the spring the grounds would be dotted with small children sprinting around like so many fawns, gathering like magic at the sight of her car, but now they were all inside. Elaine scribbled a note to remind herself to see if the welfare check could be raised to permit warmer clothing so the children could play outside in cold weather. She brought with her a little shopping bag. Mrs. Parmalee was waiting by the door to open and close it swiftly when Elaine came near.

Her smile was as warm and broad as the potbellied stove in the kitchen, which Elaine headed for to warm her hands. The children came clattering down the stairs with greetings for her. The smell of good soup hung thick and heavy in the kitchen that tripled as sitting and dining room. The smallest boy fumbled knowingly in Elaine's pocket while she smiled at his search for the tiny Chiclet boxes she carried.

"Pink," he crowed, doling out the boxes to each of the other six children who swarmed around. "Thanks, Miss Forrest, that's the goodest of all."

"Best," his mother corrected while Elaine patted the brown cheek puffed out in a smile. The mellow voice refuted her reproachful words that Miss Forrest would spoil them yet.

"They're the best-behaved and least-spoiled children I know," Elaine exclaimed, longing to be able to write out a check for the family. But pride would make Mrs. Parmalee refuse it. With her sewing she could always make out some way or other, she would say gently, calmly; and now her eldest boy was helping Jake Biddle on the garbage haul and bringing in some money each week, and Suzie was learning to do real nice skirts and aprons which they could sell.

Yes, Mr. Biddle had been up all week end, working on the place, and he was bringing them a big, fat roast for a Christmas dinner in the afternoon. He was a good man to have around, she told Elaine appreciatively, always gentle and kind with the children. He had nailed boards across the north windows so the wind didn't whistle through the house like it used to.

The children had drifted upstairs and Elaine could hear a soft chattering from the open rooms above. Once in a while a voice would be raised and then Suzie's voice would be heard, a calm, authoritative echo of her mother's, "No, you can't have Ginnie's doll; Mama said she can take it to the hospital with her. Now give it back."

"You'll have a cup of hot chocolate, Miss Forrest? I was making some for the children." Mrs. Parmalee poured out two cups and brought them to the table. Stirring her own, with head lowered, she said, "Mr. Biddle has applied for some free land on Long Island. He's part Indian, you know. He wants to build a little house for us there in the spring and start a new business. He wants to marry me." She lifted her eyes to Elaine's with a tender smile for the absurdity and gallantry of it. "But I don't know, seems like seven children's a terrible lot for a man to acquire so sudden-like." Her voice left an inquiry in the air.

"But he's devoted to you and you're fond of him, aren't you?" Elaine said. "And he's known you since before your husband died, and is fond of the children. It would be wonderful for all of you, I should think. I know you've managed awfully well alone against odds but wouldn't it be grand to . . ."

The smallest boy, who had been a silent eavesdropper on the stairs, came running to his mother with a glowing brown face. "Mr. Biddle going to be our real Daddy, Mama?"

"Why, mannikin, you mustn't listen to private talks," his mother said, but her arm went around him and lifted him to her lap. She laid her cheek against his. "Maybe so, Roger honey."

Elaine made ready to leave. "Don't worry about Ginnie's going to the hospital. The ambulance is coming Monday, and she'll be in excellent hands. She may not need an operation at all to close the heart valve if the tests don't bear out the tentative diagnosis. If an operation is needed, the county will pay the expenses, and she'll come out of it in much better health. You haven't had any flu symptoms that I can see—we'll cross our fingers that it won't happen, shall we?"

She rose and then remembered the shopping bag. "Oh, I hope you won't mind, Mrs. Parmalee, but I did want to leave a few little things for the children's Christmas, and they're in that bag all wrapped for them." She called up to the children, "Have a Merry Christmas," and they peeped down the stairway with a chorus of Merry Christmases.

She really should not show partiality in her work, but she had been unable to resist buying half a dozen Little Golden Books for the smaller children, a *Treasury of Children's Literature*, a box of Lincoln logs, a collection of plastic animals from the dime store, and a pretty, warm wool blanket. Treats were not so common in the Parmalee household, and Elaine had confidence that Mrs. Hagstrom would view the slight departure from professional policy with an indulgent eye.

There was one more stop to check on another flu patient, little Christopher in the fine stone Wiley house on Clinton Avenue. He still looked wan, but Elaine told him that if he kept warm, his mother might let him up for the family gathering in the afternoon, and his eyes sparkled again; he whispered that he thought he'd seen a new rockinghorse in his mother's closet.

Elaine went back to the Flandrau house, changed into the lovely turquoise-colored slipper-satin dress that she had bought on her New York week end, spent a pleasant hour with Mrs. Flandrau and Cora, and was pleased to hear that there had been a note with a Christmas card from Carlos Milliet that he hoped to see Mrs. Flandrau in the spring when he would come to New York on an economic mission from Argentina to the United Nations.

She put in a call to her father at their apartment and at his club without any response, so she asked the operator to try again an hour later and call her at the O'Brien's number. It would be too disappointing not to be able to talk with her father and wish him a Merry Christmas. It didn't surprise her too much that no packages had arrived from Chicago; her father was never very efficient about such things and they would probably arrive a week late.

A taxi drove away as she parked her car in front of the O'Brien house. Connie answered the door herself after an interval and welcomed her with a kiss.

"Don't you look stunning, my dear," she said, taking Elaine's coat and admiring the new dress. "Come in and see our present for you; it's life-size."

Her father had just finished stooping over an armful of presents and turned with a broad smile for his daughter.

"Daddy! No wonder I couldn't reach you!" She ran into his arms and flung her own around his neck. "Oh, Merry Christmas, Merry, Merry Christmas! I never thought you could be pried from Chicago, Daddy."

"I had to work fast." He grinned at her. "When you said you'd spend the afternoon with the O'Briens I called the airport right away, got tickets for a morning flight into New York and back this evening to Chicago, called Doc to say he'd have a guest today, and that was it." He frowned suddenly in his fearsome legal mien. "Elaine, what is this with you and Bryce? He was so evasive when I talked with him. And he's a teacher now. What is this all about?"

Elaine's happiness measurably abated. "Well, you might as well all know: we're not getting married."

"Elaine! Why ever not? You haven't quarreled, have you?"

"No, it's just that—well, of course we're still friends, but we've found out a marriage wouldn't work for us. That's all." It didn't sound so bad after all, this announcement she had dreaded to make. It was done and it hadn't been the end of the world.

In the flurry of excitement over the short visit, Elaine forgot all about the Logan album until after dinner when her father was about to leave to catch his plane. But she kept silent, uncertain whether to intrude the past into this celebration, and decided it might be too depressing to him. She kissed him good-by at the station and tried to tell him how happy his visit had made her, but he huffed with the embarrassment he showed at any display of emotion, so she only laughed and said, "Well, don't pretend it meant nothing; I know how you dread flying. It was little short of a miracle that you came."

CHAPTER ELEVEN

Elaine never relished her visits to the Vlaskas. The five children always had smudged, sullen faces; the mother was querulous, impatient, and complaining about her husband's laziness—if he didn't find work, why couldn't he begin adding another room to the shack like he'd promised when the twins were born?—and she would pull fretfully at the horrible hard curls eternally fastened to her skull with bobby pins.

Sure enough, the five-month-old twins were suffering from colds and runny noses, and two of the children were home from school with colds. The heat in the tiny kitchen was stifling and the living room was drafty. Elaine examined the children, found no fever, and said they could return to school the next day. There was a stifling, sick odor about the house—the unpleasant airlessness of many bodies cooped up in a tiny space. Even the puppy that crawled under the shabby mohair sofa looked undernourished and miserable.

"I'm glad you put the lye and disinfectant out of Johnny's reach," Elaine said to Mrs. Vlaska. On her last visit she had snatched the three-year-old away from a close inspection of the bottle of lye, and the near-accident had convinced Mrs. Vlaska when all of Elaine's patient attempts to educate her in safety precautions had failed. "Do you think Mr. Vlaska could bring you and the twins to the Child Health Clinic next week? I'd like the doctor to check on the twins again."

"Mebbe."

Mr. Vlaska lounged in, spoke a curt hello, and stood waiting for Elaine to leave. She finished washing up, said good-by, and with relief walked down the hill to the shack where the Pulaskis lived. There was a cheerful greeting from round-faced, stout little Mary Pulaski and an eager display of her infant's steady churning of chubby legs and arms. Yes, a neighbor would bring her to the clinic next week. Yes, there was the little gate her husband had put up so the two-year-old wouldn't fall down the basement steps. No, she wasn't overdoing work; the flu had touched her very lightly and she felt fine.

At the next house she had a call from the office: Please report to the Rustad house; the boys were all running a high temperature and it might be Asian flu.

The three boys were unwontedly quiet when Elaine stopped in. They all looked flushed and glazed in the eyes, and their temperatures ranged from 101 to 103. Their heads ached and they had chills and abdominal distention. Elaine phoned and left a message for Doc to call as soon as he returned.

"Asian flu, I suppose," Mrs. Rustad sighed, matter-of-fact about her tribulations.

"No, I don't think so," Elaine said, "but I want Dr. O'Brien to diagnose the case."

"Wonder if it's the same thing Annie Dunne has. She was over this morning to borrow Mr. Rustad's ax, said she had to chop some more wood. She looked pretty poorly to me, but you know her, stubborn old coot; said she hadta have more wood and wasn't going to be bothered with no doctors and nurses snooping around telling her what to do. I swear she had a fever then, Miss Forrest."

"I'd better have a look at her while I'm here. If I'm not back soon, ask Doc when he calls to drop around there too. Keep your little girl out of the boys' room; whatever it is, she might not catch it."

Elaine knocked on Annie's door but got no answer. There were no lights on, although it was a dark day. She tried the door and found it open, so she entered and switched on a light. The cats came to rub her legs, mewing loudly, and she thought she heard something moving in the bedroom. Her flashlight picked out a light bulb and when she switched it on, she saw Annie lying on the bed still clothed and breathing heavily. It was evident from her flushed face that she had a high fever.

Annie half woke while Elaine took her temperature—it was over 103—and mumbled, "They died . . . poor things." She shivered and Elaine pulled a blanket over her, wondering if this was some new epidemic on top of the other. Chills, fever, distended abdomen, the same symptoms the Rustad boys had. Who had died? What did Annie mean?

Elaine piled more wood to rekindle the fire, not very effectually until she brought some old newspapers and rearranged the logs. Something seemed different in the living room; and when the fire was finally leaping up with a crackle of papers and kindling wood, she stood up and looked uneasily around. Her glance roved over the worn sofa, the hutch table and caned chairs, the Colonial breakfront, past the bird cage in the corner to the quaint harmonium—and back to the bird cage. That was it; there was no movement. When she came closer she saw the little chartreuse and green bodies huddled together, limp and lifeless. That was what Annie meant, poor things.

The birds came from the Rustads; the Rustad boys fell sick; and now Annie was very ill. Elaine's recollection of textbook passages about psittacosis was limited, but she thought parakeets were certainly carriers. It just might be. She thought it best to do nothing but keep Annie well covered until Doc arrived to make a tentative diagnosis. She called the Rustads to see if Doc had come yet; he had already examined the boys and was on his way over.

Minutes later Doc was shedding his overcoat on the chair in Annie's bedroom and bending over her with a stethoscope. He completed a swift examination and straightened up.

"Could it be psittacosis, Doctor?"

He gave Elaine a surprised look. "That's what I think. Have you run across any cases before? It's not very commonly diagnosed any more, but I've an idea there have been quite a few unrecognized cases of parrot fever since they lifted the ban on importing parakeets."

Elaine explained the reasons for her guess.

Doc nodded. "That would do it, of course. Not knowing about the parakeets, I was puzzled at what might be the carrier. I thought it might be the chickens on the farm because they've been found to be infected in many areas—also ducks, gulls, pigeons. It can appear in any bird anywhere, but we've ceased to be alarmed about it because psittacosis lends itself well to treatment, and a severe attack is uncommon. Some people have it without realizing it. I'm not even sending the boys to the hospital, just giving them a dose of penicillin. But Annie's in worse shape—better call an ambulance right away. Good thing she's not conscious enough to battle or she'd insist she could manage alone somehow."

When Elaine finished the phone call, Doc was rolling down his sleeves and fastening the cuffs. "Next thing is to trace the parakeets and find out whether other birds are infected and have spread the disease. That might be a big job."

"Can I help? About tracing the birds or anything?"

"You certainly can, and it'll be a good experience in epidemiology for you. First we alert all the public health nurses and doctors in the county for any suspicious cases—they may have been mistakenly diagnosed as pneumonia, for instance. Then find out about the parakeets, trace them to the shops they come from, to the jobbers who sent them, the dealers who bred them, and so on. It's a long business."

"There was a sale on parakeets and canaries at the Krause Department Store in town," Elaine remembered. "Just before Christmas, I think."

"That may be it. Find out from Mrs. Rustad where they came from. In the morning we'll get a little further."

It wasn't so simple. Mrs. Rustad's sister, who lived twenty miles away, had given the birds to the children but was off on a skiing vacation in Canada. Mrs. Rustad didn't remember at what resort but gave Elaine the name of her brother-in-law's firm.

Most of the next morning Elaine spent on the phone sending wires and making long-distance calls. She finally located the couple, spoke to them long-distance, and learned that the birds had come from a pet shop in their town. She notified Dr. O'Brien and arranged to meet him at the other town in the afternoon.

On the way she stopped at Krause's store. Several dozen birds were perched in cages not far from the lunchroom counters. The clerk was at first uncooperative, and reluctant to call Mr. Krause, but a few words with Mr. Krause settled the matter at once. In his alarm at the possibility of finding infected birds, he gave full cooperation and at Elaine's advice isolated the birds in a hallway where there would be minimal contact with people. He promised to keep them distant from the lunchroom.

He gave her names of purchasers, most of whom had charge accounts or had the birds delivered, gave her addresses and phone numbers, and checked personnel records to see if any employees had shown suspicious symptoms. Two had been out since the arrival of the birds with what had been diagnosed as pneumonia: one a dishwasher, the other a girl who had attended the birds.

When Elaine met Dr. O'Brien at the pet shop in the afternoon he was pleased with her initiative. "That's using your head. I planned to get over there this afternoon. Saves me a lot of trouble and you must have handled it well to get such cooperation."

Some dozen birds came from the same jobber who had shipped to the Krause store. The proprietor of the shop was equally alarmed at the prospects of bad publicity and offered cooperation.

"Elaine," Doc said, "I think I'll leave you to take blood sample from all the birds for laboratory analysis, and I'll put you in charge of interviewing all purchasers and their doctors in case of reported illness. Mrs. Hagstrom will see that someone helps you, maybe one of her volunteer aides. I'll make out a report to the Health Department Bureau of Epidemiology for the state. Let's hope we've caught it in time to avert any serious cases."

It was hard work and took longer than Elaine had expected, and she was grateful that the flu epidemic had tapered off. She learned to be diplomatic in her contacts in order not to alarm them and to enlist their full cooperation. A few were suspicious and antagonistic, as if they feared censure for unwitting exposure to the disease. In some cases Elaine was able to get better information from the family doctor.

Nine of the birds in the two stores proved to be infected; four recovered. The birds traced from Florida dealers were the only ones affected. Elaine notified the jobbers and dealers to report any case of infected birds to local authorities.

In the households interviewed she found eighteen suspicious cases in which a member of the household developed chills, fever, and a cough after buying a parakeet or a canary. One, a small child, had an acute case but recovered quickly. Another was a father who was ill and toxic for three weeks and later suffered a relapse; Elaine had to keep in touch with the family for weeks afterward. Annie Dunne recovered slowly, but at last she was well enough to be released from the hospital.

The experience was fascinating to Elaine and she felt she had learned a great deal more about another aspect of public health, but she was happy to slide back into her former schedule and deal once again with her accustomed patients.

In the interval Mrs. Rogers had begun to spend part of her days downstairs with the children. This relieved her daughter-in-law for other chores and permitted her the freedom to shop more easily, and the tension between the two had noticeably lessened. Two or three old acquaintances of Mrs. Rogers, members of the Senior Citizens' Club, quite often came to see her; but what tickled Mrs. Rogers most was that the scribbled notes Elaine typed had turned into very respectable-looking and organized pages of print.

The old lady viewed the sheets with awe. "My goodness, I feel like a real live-and-kicking author."

"Have you some new notes for me?"

"Well, I did but I won't have to bother you with them any more. Mrs. Doyle said she'd type them for me. Says her club is gathering material for a local history book and they want everything they can lay their hands on."

"How exciting," Elaine said, and meant it. "A friend of mine, Mrs. Serrill, has been doing a series for the *Clarion*——"

"That's it, that's what gave them the idea. People got so interested in her articles that the editor hit on the notion of collecting firsthand recollections from us oldsters. And I'm one-up on them because you started me off earlier, so durned if they don't want to see how I went about it." She rocked back and forth in her chair with enormous satisfaction and then leaned forward. "Even my daughter-in-law is impressed."

"I couldn't be more pleased. You know you look ten years younger? You have color in your cheeks again."

"Oh, I'm right spry these days." She raised her voice and called into the kitchen, "Marion, how about a cup of coffee or tea for Miss Forrest?"

"I wish I could stay, Mrs. Rogers, but I have too many calls to catch up with. May I take a rain check on that?"

"Sure, sure. Just wanted you to know we're awful glad to see you."

Elaine's next stop was at the Thompson house. Hugh Thompson opened the door for her and appeared quite sober, in fact glum. From upstairs came Mrs. Hanson's shrill, peremptory voice. "Hugh, who's there? Come up and tell me. And bring my lunch, I'm hungry."

"It's the nurse," he called from the foot of the stairs. "I'll have your lunch ready soon."

"Is Mrs. Thompson around?" Elaine asked.

"She'll be home soon," he said vaguely. "Why don't you go up since you know Mother's room. I'll be along, shortly." He ran a hand through his shock of curly hair and hesitantly added, "I don't know, Rosalind got so fed up with waiting on her mother, she felt she had to clear out, see some friends. I said I'd look after Mother."

He looked so weary that Elaine felt sorry for him and offered to help with the lunch. He had set a tray with silver and a napkin and assembled a tunafish salad on lettuce leaves. Coffee was percolating on the gas stove. Elaine sliced a tomato and added potato chips and a roll.

"You look tired," she said, pouring out the coffee. "You'd better have a cup yourself first." She set it on the breakfast table before him and was touched at the appreciation in his eyes. It occurred to her that perhaps his wife's solicitude was entirely devoted to her mother these days.

"Please join me." Before she could stop him, he had gone to the stove and poured a second cup. There was something very courtly and appealing in his manner.

"I'm afraid we owe you a few dollars for your last visits," he muttered.

"There's no hurry if you're pressed," she assured him.

"Well, at the moment . . . I lost my job a couple of weeks ago, but tomorrow I have an interview for something promising."

The voice shrilled again and Hugh jumped up guiltily to get the tray. Elaine followed him upstairs. Half an hour later she was washing up when Rosalind Thompson came running up the stairs to her mother's room.

"Oh, hello, Miss Forrest, how have you been? Mother, did Hugh get you everything you need? Hugh, where's the hot-water bottle? . . . It's cold. I bought you a little present, Mother, a magazine you can read when you're tired of TV."

She sat on the bed and chattered gaily with her mother, and Elaine could detect no signs of impatience except when she addressed her husband, echoing her mother's tone, peremptory, querulous, and curt. Apparently Rosalind's excursion had relieved her spirits, but Hugh could use a little morale-building and she was doing quite the opposite. And each time Hugh shrank in her esteem, his ego suffered and his self-confidence sank another notch. No wonder it was hard for him to find another job, Elaine thought.

An unpleasant taste lingered after she left the house, but this time she was viewing the situation a little differently, with more sympathy for the husband and child, and with a suspicion that Rosalind's martyred care of her mother screened, rather poorly, her neglect of her husband and son. No, a nursing home for the mother was no answer until Rosalind and Hugh could place the mother in a proper perspective, as a guest in the home instead of the central character, dominating the household from her invalid's bed. What was the key to the situation? Was it the son? Could Hugh's responsibility toward the boy make him assert himself more as a man? That might supply the motivation. She decided to talk it over again with Frieda.

Mrs. Flandrau called to Elaine when she entered the house after dinner. "Elaine? Do come in, I've heard again from my friend Carlos. He expects to be here late in March and I want you to meet him."

Elaine noted the same thrill at feeling once more related and wanted, that she had seen that morning in Mrs. Rogers' face— a restoration to life existing around her from which she had felt cut off. This ailment of loneliness had existed before, but it was only recently that the chord of sympathy had been plucked in Elaine so that she understood something of the isolation of the elderly. It was her own solitude and loneliness this winter that had provided the clue to what had once only baffled and irritated her.

"Oh, how very nice, Mrs. Flandrau. Is it long since you've seen him?"

"Many years, my dear. He and his family had a bad time during the Perón regime, but now that it's over, they're becoming prominent and active again. He's thinking of entering the diplomatic corps. Oh, dear, I nearly forgot. Cora left a letter for you in your room; she called for the mail this afternoon when she was in town." There was a twinkle in her eyes. "From her manner I judged the letter might be from your young Mr. Thorne."

There was a pause, during which the twinkle in the knowledgeable old eyes changed to concern. "There isn't anything wrong, is there, Elaine?" and Elaine knew that her expression must have hinted at her fleeting impulse to confess that Bryce was no longer her young man.

"Oh, no, nothing wrong," she smiled, and escaped from the room before she could yield to that impulse.

Mounting the stairs, she wondered why she found it so hard to speak of the break. After New Year's Bryce had sent her a friendly letter, which in some ways seemed more revealing than the previous short notes. He was in his element teaching, and wrote her at length about his work and some of his students. It was heartening to feel that their relationship was still close, and she wrote him an appreciative answer with more awareness of his interests and needs. Since then his letters had continued to come in a new vein of friendliness without emotional overtones. She hardly knew whether it helped or hurt to continue the correspondence.

With the unopened letter in her hand she stood at the window and watched the snow floating down. What was that line . . . "Now is the winter of our discontent . . ." Well, she was plunk in the middle of it. Still, was it so bad? Something had destroyed her vision of the future, but she had had too little leisure recently to feel the privation.

She had been determined to face herself honestly, and yet part of that must be to end the masquerade as Bryce's fiancée before Mrs. Flandrau and Cora. Did she still have hopes of a reconciliation? Was it that she couldn't yet bear to acknowledge except to Kitty the fact that she had been, as Dirk so bluntly put it, jilted? Pride must still be dominant if she could not face her friends without duplicity.

There always came a time for decision, and decision was never easy. With a sigh she slit open the letter and glanced through it. Some references to an evening with her father, some talk about a new project at school, mention of mutual friends, and then a paragraph at the end that made her gasp.

"This may seem odd to you, Elaine, but I hope it will not be too neglectful of your feelings if I make a request of you. You may remember that last fall Kitty Gullen had spoken of a visit to her brother in Chicago during a winter vacation, and of course I had asked her to call when she came. It occurs to me that if she knows about our breaking the engagement she might feel some hesitancy or delicacy about getting in touch with me, and I really would like to see her. As you can imagine, now that I am getting into the swing of things at school, I'm beginning to have a little more leisure and would welcome some activity to fill the void, so to speak.

"Would it hurt you if I did see her? If not, perhaps you could find some way of letting her know about us, of making her feel that there is no disloyalty involved. I think that for her as well as for me, loyalty to you and regard for your feelings would be the first consideration. I'll leave it entirely to you . . ."

So always there was some new hurdle, some fresh pain. The implication percolated painfully. Dirk had seen it plainly, but even now when it was down in writing, Elaine could hardly accept the idea. How stupid not to have known it before. It fitted in with Kitty's depression after Bryce left, with Bryce's new firmness about his career, and yet she knew that Bryce was right; they would both set loyalty before their inclinations.

There was still resistance within Elaine. She set her own intelligence, background, appearance, and education against Kitty's. What had Kitty to offer, a girl from a common family and background and education—how could she fit in with Bryce's breeding, family position, and wealth? She gave her head a toss, trying to shake off this residue of snobbery and ego, but it wasn't that easy.

"Miss Forrest? May I come in?" That was Cora tapping at the door.

Elaine sat up, on the verge of refusing, and then changed her mind. "Yes, Cora, do come in. I wanted to thank you for cleaning my coat," she added.

"I made some brownies this afternoon and thought you might like some before you went to bed," Cora said. She set down a tray with a steaming pot of hot chocolate and a cup with a marshmallow in it. "You've been so busy these last few weeks that I think you've lost weight."

"Oh, Cora," murmured Elaine. She bit into one of the brownies. "Ummm. Delicious. I wouldn't have thought I was hungry after a big dinner, but I am." She sipped her hot chocolate and thought how unobtrusive and how cheering Cora's solicitude was; she knew how to reach through loneliness and say by her actions that she cared and wanted to help. It wasn't merely selflessness, it was a kind of blossoming.

While Cora moved around the room straightening furniture, window blinds, bedspread, anything a trifle out of place, Elaine thought of Kitty. This warmth and understanding Kitty and Cora held in common, a sensitivity to the needs of others, and each responded in different but equally effective ways. Was it something Elaine could learn herself? Mrs. Hagstrom had it; Molly Carew had it. No wonder they were marvelous nurses. And marvelous people.

A wave of disillusionment swept over her when Cora said good night and closed the door. The bitterness of Bryce's letter ebbed and left her limp with hopelessness and humility. Was she a failure both as a person and as a nurse? Maybe that was what Dirk had sensed and had made him withdraw so readily.

The memory of Miss Schwartz floated into her mind and puzzled her until she grasped a clue. There was no denying her effectiveness as a nurse, and she seemed to Elaine one of the least attractive people, forbidding, glum, and unresponsive; and yet she was a rock of security and assurance. Her record as a nurse was unrivaled even by Molly. That must mean something. Perhaps you didn't have to conform to some idealized pattern or be socially attractive to find satisfaction in your work and an effective role in life. Miss Schwartz was firmly and undeviatingly and triumphantly herself and knew herself to be effective and useful and valued. That was her secret.

If Miss Schwartz could be an individual—and she was monumentally that—and a force by dint of being herself to the hilt, then maybe Elaine could accept herself for what she was and do the best with her own temperament, whatever its faults.

Whatever its faults . . . Strange to think of herself apologetically after all these years, a young lifetime of taking her good fortune and gifts for granted.

Well, she had better learn to take the strong steps that would bring back a sense of self-respect. She sat down at the desk and began a letter to Bryce. It was hard to send approval and to say she would make sure Kitty called him. She did it with full recognition that Bryce was not a man to dabble in affections and that with the evidence of Kitty's response to him, it was not beyond the realm of probability that Kitty might one day occupy the status as Bryce's wife that Elaine had so long anticipated for herself. And she did it as generously as she could.

CHAPTER TWELVE

March was drawing to a close and Elaine noted eagerly the signs of spring. Driving along the roads, she spotted a bright bit of yellow or purple blossom where the crocuses peeped up; the willows were turning green-gold; the lilac bushes were forming tiny buds; and the trees now appeared faintly lacy, with buds softening their silhouette. And with spring came a rush of well-being.

Kitty had spent her week in Chicago, returning with a fresh glow and an account of late-afternoon walks with Bryce through Lincoln Park, a visit to the zoo, a visit with Bryce to Elaine's father, a meeting with Bryce's family at a rather formal and formidable dinner, a play, an opera—all carefully matter-of-fact and tailored for Elaine's sensitive ears. It hurt less than Elaine would have thought.

Between the lines of Kitty's account she could discern a developing relationship with Bryce that might alarm his family. But she could guess the winning effect of Kitty's presence, the gradual succumbing and thawing to her charm and range of experience, and a tacit admission that the family would withdraw its opposition. And there was a certain relief at Bryce's tact in avoiding their favorite old haunts, certain restaurants and spots like Jacques', the Allerton, The Buttery, as if he were safeguarding what remained of their links.

Dirk's attitude continued to puzzle and confuse Elaine. She

often had the feeling, in the midst of a conference, that he was studying her, and she resented the idea of being evaluated. There were times when he came upstairs for some information from the files or from one of the nurses when she suspected his motivation was to be near her. And if he stopped at her desk to discuss the Thompsons with her, she again had a hovering sense of expectation and yet uncertainty too. She was never sure whether she dreaded or enjoyed those brief encounters, but she was always conscious of his footsteps on the stairs, of his eyes on her from the door. But he never asked to see her after work. Once when the other nurses were late getting back to the office, she thought he was on the verge of it, but Frieda's rubber-soled approach interrupted.

The inconclusiveness of what should have been concluded bothered Elaine, and she almost wished there would be another incident so that she could air her irritation. But there was nothing to provide the excuse.

Frieda Manship's behavior had been peculiar lately, and Kitty had said in her tolerant way that it was because her mother was seriously ill and Frieda herself was exhausted. She and Frieda had already discussed the Thompson case, yet one day Frieda overheard Dirk talking to Elaine about the family, and she became overfriendly and suggested that she ought to accompany Elaine on a visit.

At any other time Elaine would have agreed immediately, but she had a notion that this was a critical point in the Thompson case and was anxious not to intrude any new factor. Hugh had gotten a new job and seemed to have acquired a fresh degree of control and self-respect. He had found time to paint the outside of the house and had celebrated by taking Rosalind to New York for dinner and a play. This was clearly not approved by the mother, who probably sensed the beginning of a loss of influence and she showed it by making more peremptory demands than ever.

Frieda became so insistent, that Elaine reluctantly consented to take her the following week, possibly the day after the conference. By then Elaine hoped the Thompsons would be secure in their new pattern through which Rosalind could shake off her sense of guilt about her mother's illness and care for her without centering her whole life around the invalid to the detriment of her husband and child.

When Elaine slipped into the conference room and took the chair next to Frieda, Frieda accorded her a short nod and a disgruntled smile. Elaine wondered what was wrong with her now and hoped it wasn't bad news about the invalid mother.

There was talk first of a safety campaign in the schools to make the children and their families more aware of hazards in the home and the need for safety measures.

"Oh, remember a project that was reported in the *Journal of Public Health Nursing* not long ago? They ran a contest in the schools in which the children made dioramas in shoeboxes of a visiting nurse situation." Kitty frowned in an attempt to recall the date. "A few months ago I think. Couldn't we use that idea as a basis for safety campaigns in the local schools?"

The matter was settled, and there followed the usual parade of cases that required the benefit of collective judgment and experience. Elaine's amputee, Mr. Spiotti, was one of the cases. Both she and Phil Roland believed that the old man, now in his mid-seventies, had profited so much from the series of exercises Phil had given him, and was so eager to be fitted for an artificial leg, that he should have one. The Welfare Department in most cases involving a man of his age was disinclined to provide the considerable sum for a prosthetic limb, but Dr. O'Brien agreed that in this case the extra expense was justified and he made a note to send a recommendation to that effect.

Elaine leaned back, pleased and relieved. Dr. O'Brien crossed off the Spiotti name from the agenda, frowned at the next item, and jerked his head up. He looked annoyed.

"Frieda, do you want to explain a little more about your concern for the Thompson family? You seem to think matters are getting much worse there. Well?"

Surprised, Elaine looked at Frieda, who stood up and cleared her throat. How could Frieda have anything to say about the Thompsons when Elaine hadn't even taken her there yet?

"Of course I realize that ordinary procedure calls for the nurse to consult me and invite suggestions, but I gathered from what has been said at previous conferences that conditions at the Thompson house are at a serious stage and I felt it my duty as the qualified social worker on the staff . . ."

Did Elaine imagine it or was there a biting crispness about Frieda's enunciation of those words that was intended as a slur on Dirk's presence and project? Dirk's face was impassive; she could not tell whether he felt the slur or not.

". . . to satisfy myself that the family in question was not simply being treated like guinea pigs, but was getting all necessary attention. I spoke to Miss Forrest about it last week and received most evasive answers. It worried me so that I took matters into my own hands and visited the Thompsons myself on Friday."

A slow fire began to smolder inside Elaine and she could see Dirk flushing a dark red.

"If you remember, Frieda, we were to go together this week; there was no reason—or need—for you to go alone," Elaine said in a carefully restrained voice. "As I explained then, it was a crucial time, and I hoped it would be a turning point for the whole family, and any appearance of another observer then I felt was unwise. You might trust me to call you in when circumstances warranted it."

Ignoring her, Frieda continued to address Dr. O'Brien and Mrs. Hagstrom. "I'm sure Miss Forrest had every good intention," she said silkily, "but unfortunately not every nurse is qualified to meet all the needs of her cases. Miss Forrest tends, for instance, to maintain impersonal relations with her patients and therefore is not in close contact with their human needs, although she is obviously well qualified in the medical aspects of her work. I recall that she has even proclaimed that she has set herself a minimum number of calls per day, as if she rationed each visit——"

An audible gasp emerged from Kitty during the startled silence that attended Frieda's onslaught. It was so unexpected, such a gross breach of medical ethics, etiquette, and good working morale in the office, and yet so craftily subdued, that the prevailing reaction was one of entire astonishment and disbelief.

Trying desperately to keep her head and her temper, Elaine addressed herself to Mrs. Hagstrom. "Mrs. Hagstrom, I don't know why Frieda is magnifying this to such momentous proportions. It's true that she spoke to me last week about the case and I was reluctant then, but we did agree to make a call together this week. It's also true, I regret to say, that when I first came here I had some very naïve ideas about my duties, and unfortunately I did make some foolish remarks that I'm ashamed of now. I didn't realize then the complexity of the work or understand how illness relates to the home, the family, the community, the whole environment. I admit freely that both Frieda and Dirk have been responsible for a change in my attitude, and I believe you'll find that my records reflect this change and an eff——"

Frieda broke in triumphantly, "You see, she admits it! Naturally I've been reluctant to criticize a colleague . . ."

Dr. O'Brien's little beard bristled and he snapped, "Frieda, you had better be very careful what you say! This kind of accusation can lead to a very bad reputation."

"I hope I have a deeper sense of my obligations than to play safe and permit criminal negligence toward patients," Frieda retorted. "I realize that Miss Forrest is a protégé of yours, but when I found Mrs. Thompson in such a state that she might have committed murder by withholding the proper medica——"

"Murder! Criminal negligence!" Dirk's self-control burst. "Mrs. Hagstrom, Dr. O'Brien, I've been in very close touch with the Thompson family for several months now and I can assure you that this charge about Mrs. Thompson is sheer nonsense. I saw them the day after Frieda's visit and except for the fact that she herself upset them——"

"Of course he'd say that," Frieda cried. "Don't you see, he's defending—defending . . ." A bewildered look crossed her face and she pressed a hand against her forehead, pushing back a lock of hair. "Oh, yes, defending his thesis and his notions about family diagnosis. And he's covering up for Miss Forrest too . . ."

"Frieda Manship, he's not covering up for me or for anybody else! Mrs. Thompson's mother has always been resistant to medication and——"

"Stop this, all of you!" Mrs. Hagstrom stood up, outraged. "I never witnessed such behavior. Are you children or are you professional people? This conference is over. Frieda, Elaine, Dirk, I want you to remain."

A hush descended on the room as one by one the other nurses and Phil Roland departed. Dr. O'Brien looked inquiringly at Mrs. Hagstrom, ready to intervene, but she shook her head. "This is my responsibility, Doctor. I must apologize for letting my staff reach such a stage. I shall have to get to the bottom of it. I'm terribly sorry you've been exposed to this unpleasant scene."

Elaine's heart was hammering wildly. Surely Mrs. Hagstrom didn't imagine that there was any substance to the accusation! Frieda must be mad! Elaine's mind raced over the details of her talk with Frieda, over snatches she might have overheard of talks with Dirk. Other unpleasant recollections crowded in, remarks Frieda had made now and then about coldness, about self-centered women, about keeping people at arm's length. Elaine realized now that these had been aimed at her. There had been other sly remarks about Dirk fancying himself as a social worker and interfering in what was none of his business. She had dismissed these things as general office griping, but now it seemed that Frieda had deliberately tried to set the stage for a scene, deliberately tried to turn everyone against Elaine and Dirk.

In Mrs. Hagstrom's little office the atmosphere was distinctly frosty. The three of them were silent while Mrs. Hagstrom sat at her desk staring down at a pile of papers, tapping her fingers, drumming on the desk.

At last she said abruptly, "I'm terribly displeased about this performance. Frieda, if anything is drastically wrong, you should talk to me first, not air your opinions in a general conference without any supporting evidence. There is a possibility, you know, that you might be mistaken. And Elaine and Dirk, I'm surprised at your behavior too. On second thought, this is no time to speak about it; tempers are too high."

The clock ticked loudly in the silent room. "I want each of you to devote the rest of the afternoon to writing a complete report of your version of the conditions of the Thompson family and your prognosis, supported by all pertinent evidence in the records. Facts, not theories. Once that is done, the matter should be a little clearer and perhaps we can determine with less bias what the facts are and what should be done. I want those reports in tonight. After I've read them and had a chance to consider, I shall see each of you individually. Is that clear? Are there any questions?"

The office was deserted when Elaine went up to her typewriter. Through the closed door that separated Frieda's tiny office in the back from the large room, she could hear the spasmodic chatter of the typewriter, then silence, then an impatient scrape of a chair, a nervous pacing, another staccato sound of typing.

In an attempt to bring the whole picture into focus, Elaine blotted out everything else and sat at her desk to think out the reasons for Frieda's outburst, to get at the root of the problem in the Thompson family, to examine searchingly her own part in the whole affair.

She sat deep in thought for a long time. At last she consulted her folder on the Thompsons, studied the records, put a sheet of paper, carbon, and onionskin in her typewriter and began typing, slowly at first and then faster, more surely. By the time she finished the last page darkness had fallen. She separated the carbons from the originals, clipped the originals to her records, put on her coat, and went downstairs to leave the folder with Mrs. Hagstrom. Upstairs, Frieda's typewriter still clicked frantically. Dirk must have left; another report was already on the desk.

Mrs. Hagstrom said thank you in a noncommittal voice and Elaine walked out to the car. What a terrible blow it must be to Mrs. Hagstrom to have her staff members behave so badly, so unprofessionally, and she humbly included herself in the condemnation. Mrs. Hagstrom was so proud of the staff and their work that Elaine felt worse about that than about any other consequence.

And the consequences might be drastic. She might lose her job. And all at once Elaine was aware that it meant a great deal to her and that she very much wanted to continue in it and earn Mrs. Hagstrom's esteem. She had come to love this town, to feel an affection for her colleagues and many of her patients, and she treasured the *esprit de corps* that so strongly marked their unit.

The night brought rising winds and dark clouds that meant storm. When Elaine stopped to fill the gas tank it was snowing, and as she drove off she wondered what to do next. She had no appetite but did not feel like going home or seeing anyone. Approaching the turn-off to Annie Dunne's barn, she remembered the almost-forgotten urge to explore further. It was as good a reason as any to avoid going home.

Annie, with her own eccentricities and tolerance of idiosyncrasies, thought nothing odd about her request for permission to spend an hour or so in the barn. Elaine picked her way carefully by flashlight; the snow was slippery underfoot and she had worn no boots over her low-heeled pumps.

The wind whistled through cracks in the old barn, and the floor creaked with cold. Elaine's breath sent frost into the hard light of the suspended bulb. She found the trunk Katie had spoken of and began to search through it. Someone, Annie perhaps, had stuck batches of unrelated documents and letters in with the Logan papers and it was some time before she found anything of interest.

The first thing was a collection of maps, some old, some fairly recent, labeled "Logan Estate." The oldest map marked several hundred acres south of Kahopac. It included Winding Hill Road, which led to the Flandrau house. Consulting the other maps, she found the estate dwindling until it was farm-size in the last one. Orienting herself by the position of the lakes and the main highway, Elaine discovered that the last sale recorded the Flandrau name. Judging by the position of their house and the little brook that flowed down the hill, the house that the Serrills lived in must be the same Logan house that appeared on the first map!

This meant that the view Elaine looked out upon was almost precisely that which her mother saw as a girl from the house below. The thought of it excited her curiosity even more and made her disregard the cold to continue her search. Her fingers flew faster until near the end she almost missed the notebooks; they looked so unpromising—plain brown notebooks, the same kind that she had used for lecture notes in college. But for her mother they had been diaries.

Her teeth were chattering and she was hungry now, so she stopped for a hamburger before returning home. The snow fell thickly now and the winds were almost a gale. She drove up the hill at fifteen miles an hour and it was with relief that she turned into the familiar courtyard. She came in, shook the snow from her coat, briefly greeted Cora and Mrs. Flandrau, and ran upstairs to study her finds.

She made herself comfortable on the bed in her favorite reading position, lying on her stomach with her elbows propping her up. At first she felt disappointment as she glanced through the scrawls in the dog-eared brown notebooks, so childish, so rounded, neat, proper—and void of character. None of the informal little breaks and eccentric marks of the individual, nothing but the legible, trained, faultless, and unformed writing of a schoolgirl. And the subject matter seemed just as conventional and ordinary.

It dawned on her that she was expecting too much, a fully formed adult instead of a schoolgirl, and she began to read for potentialities, for signs of the future, for clues to character in the reading her mother had done, in her reactions to ordinary events, little excursions, midterm tests and report cards, a movie or play, a dance, an auto trip to Washington, D.C., or Boston with her parents, a week end in New York with friends, a quiet evening party given by her parents.

Elaine found poems squeezed between entries, recognized some favorite sonnets, and suspected some were original. Now the picture was emerging of a serious little ladylike girl with surprising gusts of laughter breaking through her sobriety, with an artless self-consciousness and aspiration, a tendency toward primness, an engaging naïveté.

And all at once without fanfare, a drama.

After her graduation from high school came the summer when the Flandraus built their house and found their seventeen-year-old neighbor often underfoot, curiously watching the construction work, exploring the growing innards of the house, excited as it took shape. By the time Phyllis went away to school at Vassar, the Logans and Flandraus had become friends, and on week ends at home Phyllis spent much of her time there, meeting their friends from New York or abroad. The cosmopolitan Flandraus with their lavish entertaining must have presented a glamorous contrast to the quiet father and mother who contented themselves with local society and friends.

There began small flurries of interest in some of the young men who attended the parties, a court reporter, a medical student, a pharmacist. From a snapshot loose among the pages Elaine saw a pretty blonde girl with a short pageboy bob, dark eyes that looked out with a shy innocence, and a kind of waiting-in-the-wings expression, as if she expected something extraordinary to materialize.

The next fall when Phyllis came home for Thanksgiving vacation she was spending a quiet evening with the Flandraus when there was a screeching of car tires and brakes, a slamming of doors in the entrance, and two young men erupted into the room. The taller one in his exuberance whirled Mrs.

Flandrau around with shouts of greetings in Spanish, and then introduced the shorter man with the little mustache, very good-looking and more reserved. The *gauchos* Phyllis called them. The tall one, son of friends, had come to study in New York and made friends with a young painter from Peru. They had been so busy finding an apartment and furnishing the loft they had moved into that there had been no time to call, and that afternoon they had decided to surprise the Flandraus.

An idea occurred to Elaine after Phyllis' second encounter with the *gauchos*, and she riffled through in a search for names. The diary showed it a month later when they spent Christmas with the Flandraus—Vicente Tejeros and Carlos Milliet!

It was exasperating, maddening, and comic. It was exhilarating and disturbing and impossibly coincidental and withal in some odd way inevitable and ironically satisfying. To come almost by accident to her nursing job in Kahopac, her mother's birthplace, to find lodgings in the house next to the Logan home, to discover these notebooks through a friendship with the Serrills who lived in that home, and to cultivate the friendship of the woman who had been almost a foster mother to her own!

CHAPTER THIRTEEN

Disregarding the late hour, Elaine read on. Throughout that winter the *gauchos* were always together and made a threesome with Phyllis during their visits, and it was never clear which one was closer to her. Both of them wrote her gallant little notes while she was at Vassar, both danced with her and partnered her in tennis; both sent charming, whimsical gifts at Valentine's Day and Easter; both escorted her on rare trips to New York City.

Which, *which*? Then Elaine found the episode that triggered off the drama. Vicente met Phyllis alone one morning at Grand Central; Carlos was ill with fever and dysentery and had specifically warned Vicente to continue their plans and not to bring Phyllis near him. So they went to the library, lunched in the garden of the Museum of Modern Art, strolled up Fifth Avenue, and wandered around the zoo in Central Park. Vicente talked about his home in Lima, the three-hundred-year-old high-ceilinged house, the Indian servants, his friends. Without warning, in the lightest of veins, Vicente asked, "How would you like to marry me and live in Lima?"

Phyllis laughed, unable to take him seriously, and then was embarrassed and worried that she had hurt his feelings, and tried to rescue the evening by joking with him. Suddenly she knew that if it had been Carlos instead she would not have laughed, would not have refused.

The image of Carlos kept recurring until she insisted that Vicente take her, illness or no illness, to see how he was. He looked awful in the little bedroom behind the studio in the loft. He was unshaven, his hair rumpled, his dark eyes glazed with fever, and he was alternately feverish and shaking with chills under a pile of blankets. Phyllis called a doctor she knew in New York, made cold compresses to soothe Carlos' forehead, sent Vicente out for some soup and crackers. Only when the doctor came would she leave.

For the first time Vicente and Carlos had become separate entities to her, and it was Carlos who drew her. He had looked so ridiculous and so pathetic in his anger at Vicente for letting her see him, but was too sick and miserable to do anything but succumb to her ministrations.

Next day came the report that he was better, but Carlos sounded aggrieved; his pride was hurt and he hadn't forgiven her. He wanted to be at his best for her and she had seen him at his worst. It was a month later, when school ended, that she saw them both again at the Flandraus'.

Vicente had regained his high spirits and composure, but Carlos was self-conscious and subdued. Yet when the evening was over it was he who escorted Phyllis down to her house. They lingered on the bridge and then it happened, so quietly and easily that she only half believed that it had. He kissed her and then they were talking about plans for marriage. He would continue his studies after a trip home to his family, when he would break the news. In the fall they would be married. He would finish his doctorate by the spring, and they would live in Buenos Aires and he would teach in the university. They would come back each year to visit her family and see friends.

It didn't look that simple to her parents the next morning. Phyllis was too young; she hadn't finished college; she would be too far away . . . There was a serious family talk with Carlos.

They must recognize the difficulties of marriage between young people of such different backgrounds—was Carlos sure his family would approve? Did he have funds? And what about the difference in religion that might create discords?

It was decided that they might announce their engagement, but they must wait until Phyllis had finished college and Carlos had his family's approval before marriage. Unwillingly they acknowledged that this made sense, and agreed to wait. Phyllis was terribly in love, and the cable that came two months later was a shocking interruption to their idyll.

Carlos' father was dying of cancer. In a few days Carlos was packed and ready to sail for South America. Seeing him off, Phyllis had an aching fear that she might never see him again, and there was a moment when each saw the guarded fear in the other's eyes. Then Carlos took her into his arms, kissed her with tenderness shining in his dark eyes, held his lips against the curve of her cheeks wet by tears. *"Hasta luego, mi amor, mi corazón,"* he whispered, held her close, and then strode up the gangplank without looking back.

Carlos' first letter rescued Phyllis from her moods of depression with its tenderness and its understanding of her loneliness and fears. More letters came; the illness was protracted. Months later when his father died, Carlos had to administer the complicated family affairs, and wrote to ask her to come down with her parents the following summer. But her father could not leave his business, and Phyllis suspected he looked hopefully on the separation as a prelude to ending the engagement. She had no money of her own to make the trip alone, and her father would not permit her to accept it from Carlos.

Discouraged, she also detected signs that his family resented the impending marriage. Religion, nationality, social status, and disparity in their backgrounds produced multiple obstacles. Then came a desperate letter from Carlos. Sensing her spair, he wrote that he was coming back for a short visit, and at that time wanted to arrange a wedding, help her shop and pack, and then bring her back with him to Buenos Aires.

Her response was uncertain; nevertheless he came but could not seem to convince her. Her father was in poor health and worried about his business, and she could not face a break with her parents. There was an interval of silence after Carlos went back alone and then she wrote him a long letter, a draft of which Elaine found in the notebook.

Gently and tenderly Phyllis told him how desperately she had wanted to leave with Carlos the first time. In spite of the chasm that now parted them, the chasm of time and distance, the bond between them was still so strong that she felt she had to release him so that each would feel free to love and marry someone else. She felt that while he was in the background of her life, the hope of marriage would interfere with any other attachment, and she felt it was useless to follow a mirage, a dream. And she told him her plans to go and study in Chicago.

And with that letter the notebook ended.

Too tired to take off her uniform Elaine lay on her bed enveloped in gloom and disappointment. What a let-down that such a love affair should taper off into nothing. It was as if she didn't know the ending of the story—the meeting with the successful young lawyer in Chicago and the marriage a year later. Elaine saw herself with a queer new vision. How different Phyllis' life would have been in Buenos Aires. And how could Elaine herself have come into existence? It was weird to realize that she would not have been here to read this history if that love story had followed its course, and yet she was ironically grieved and disappointed. Musing over the paradox turned into a deep sleep.

Hours later the telephone woke her. Groggily she reached for

"Good morning, my dear, I'm sure you can't attempt to go to work this morning."

"Good morning. No, Kitty phoned to tell me the office was closed. But I have some news that should interest you." Elaine's eyes sparkled with mischief. "What would you say if I told you that last night I learned a great deal about your friend Carlo Milliet? And that my mother used to sit at this very table with you at one time? And that my grandparents lived in the house below?"

Each question raised Mrs. Flandrau's eyebrows a trifle higher until she gathered Elaine's meaning. "Elaine! You mean you are the daughter of my little friend Phyllis? Why, how extraordinary! I would not have thought of it, but you do look a little bit like her—not in coloring but in facial structure. My dear Elaine! Cora, Cora, do come here!"

"Yes, Mrs. Flandrau?" Smiling at the delighted tone, Cora appeared at the door with Mrs. Flandrau's coffee and placed it on the table. Before her mistress could say more, Cora lowered her head in the direction of the window and exclaimed, "There it is again. That light at the Serrill house."

Elaine, facing the window, could see it from her chair. "Oh, I must try calling them again, I think their phone is out. Now what do you suppose . . . ? It looks like a signal, doesn't it?" Abruptly the explanation occurred to her and she ran to the window. "Has this been going on long, Cora? When did you see it first?"

"Oh, half an hour or so ago. Before you came down. What do you think it means? It might have been going on earlier, but the snow was too thick before; it's thinning out now."

Elaine ran to the telephone and dialed quickly. "Still out. Oh dear, I'll bet Katie's in labor! Why else would they be signaling?" She put fingers to her forehead. "I must get down there somehow, but I'd better tell Doc first. Cora! Get Dr. O'Brien

n the phone, tell him to rush over, that Mrs. Serrill must be
having her baby. Oh dear, how will he manage to get over with
the roads like this? Tell him Dirk's friend Matt Crawford has
a snow plow on his jeep; maybe Dirk can borrow it and get
him over. Oh, what a time for a storm! What a time to have a
baby! I'll get into my ski pants and boots and hike down as
quickly as I can. Let me know if you get through to Doc, Cora.
Be an angel?"

She darted upstairs, dragged out the carton of winter clothes
she had just packed away, and pulled out her ski outfit. In two
minutes she was ready, remembered to tuck in a flashlight, and
ran down the stairs. Cora had reached Doc and he would get in
touch right away with Dirk and Matt and hoped they'd be able
to make it in an hour or so.

"Oh, I hope all the power isn't off," Elaine said fervently.
"They have a gas stove and a fireplace anyhow. I'll be off now.
If it's a false alarm I'll try to get back quickly—no, I'll signal
twice with the flashlight in an hour. Okay, Cora?"

The blizzard had tapered off and the wind had dropped, but
it was still awkward trying to keep her balance with the black
bag under her arm. She had to take the long way, along the
road, otherwise she risked dangerous footing under the drifts.
It seemed to take forever to plow her way down the road. At
the lane the collie rushed out to greet her with a fusillade of
barks, and his floundering made a path for her that was easier
to follow. At the sound of the collie's greeting Paul came to the
door and waved. Midway down the lane a branch had fallen
from a tree and split the telephone wire; there was still hope
of power in the house then. But there was no electricity either.

Katie was in labor, had been for three hours, and Paul hadn't
dared leave her. She lay on her bed looking quite composed and
cheerful.

"I'm so glad Paul's home. He was supposed to stay in town

last night with friends, but decided to come home late instead when he saw the storm. The pains have been coming about every ten minutes."

So the birth might occur very soon, Elaine thought. It was one thing to watch or participate in a delivery in a sterilized operating room in a well-equipped hospital, and to remember with confidence old Dr. Sylvester's leisurely admonition that in a normal birth all you had to do was wait and keep the mother as relaxed as possible. It was quite another to be alone in a home with a power failure, ill-equipped, in the middle of a blizzard, the doctor miles away—and the mother-to-be one of your close friends. Elaine did not relish the prospect of an immediate delivery, and hoped it would not occur until the doctor's arrival.

"You were right to lie down until someone came," Elaine told Katie, "but now I'll have to get you up to change the sheets and put newspapers underneath. Paul, could you . . . ?"

But he had already disappeared in a hunt for papers and brought back a moundful. "And I suppose you want pots and pots of boiling water," he suggested with a grin. He paused at the door. "Since the electricity is off and the pump won't work, maybe I'd better melt snow and save what water still remains in the tank for an emergency. We have two or three big electric lamps besides this, so the light situation is under control."

Elaine smiled. "I don't have to tell you a thing, do I? Now what about a——"

"Bassinet? We bought one last month; it's in the next room. Is it warm enough here? I've kept fires going in the fireplaces since the power went off, and closed off the rooms that we won't use now."

"It's fine, just keep logs on hand to keep them going." She held Katie's hand as another pain came, then tucked her warmly into the bed. Full of trepidation herself, she could not

174

fford the luxury of a single mistake or evidence of insecurity o trouble Katie or Paul. She got clean towels from the linen closet and arranged what she needed on the dresser: sterile gloves, soap, a basin for water, a sterile towel. She began telling Katie and Paul about her discovery of the notebooks, and time passed without Katie's noticing how much closer the pains were coming now—every five minutes, every three minutes.

As she talked, Elaine's alert ears were waiting for any reassuring sounds from the road. There would be no medication and she hoped Katie would continue to take things well. Paul certainly looked more composed than most husbands would be, and kept the talk lively with his comments on Phyllis and the likelihood that Phyllis herself was born in this very room, but he, too, kept timing the pains.

A look of surprise suddenly crossed Katie's face. "Well, I guess this is it. That one was a humdinger. Paul, would you hold my hand—unless you'd rather go away?" Paul stayed, now a little pale.

It may have seemed endless to Katie, but only minutes passed before the baby's head appeared and slowly the body emerged while Elaine grasped it with gentle, firm pressure, using the sterile towel. Soon there was a cry from the baby, a girl, and after tying the umbilical cord Elaine gently cleaned the infant with a soft cloth, wrapped her in warm blankets, laid her down for a few minutes by Katie's tired, perspiring face, long enough for the mother to whisper, "Jennifer, Paul?" and smile faintly, then she put it in the bassinet. While Elaine was sponging Katie's hot face she heard the outer door open and feet stomped into the hallway.

Paul went out to see who it was, and the sound of Doc's sharp inquiries and then his booming laugh came into the bedroom. He pulled off his coat and chuckled as he rubbed his hands to-

gether. "Didn't need me after all, did you? Looks like a nic
clean job, Elaine. We'll give her a shot of penicillin as soon a
I wash up." He went on talking from the bathroom while h
washed, announcing that the snow had stopped and the high
way below was being cleared. "Some reckless creature was head
ing down the road with a big basket when we turned in. Wha
possesses people to come out in this weather when they don'
have to?"

The collie was barking in the yard and Paul went to the doo
to admit Cora, wrapped up in shawls and covered with snow
She was beaming at news of the baby girl and had brought .
basketful of cold chicken, rolls, butter, and brownies becaus
she was sure no one else had thought of food and they must b
starving; and Mrs. Flandrau had sent her and said not to com
back until she wasn't needed. She promptly set to work makin
a late lunch.

Elaine thought she was ready to collapse of exhaustion, bu
the sight of the juicy chicken reminded her that she was starv
ing. "Cora, you are a darling. And a thermos jug of coffee
and cream too." She laughed. "Oh, I can see you won't b
happy till you've seen the baby, so run into the bedroom an
take a look. Both mother and child are sleeping now. Tell Do
to come in and have a bite too. And whose is the fourth plate
Oh." She suddenly remembered Dirk had chauffeured Doc
and went to look for him.

He came in a minute later. "Thought I might as well plow
your lane for you, Paul. Call it a present for the baby." He
clapped Paul on the back and congratulated him; then stared
at Elaine. "You look tired enough to have had the baby your
self, Elaine. Are you all right? Sit down and rest." He led her
to a chair and she collapsed in it gratefully.

Paul brought out a bottle of champagne in celebration and

they toasted the new baby. Then he proposed another toast, "To Phyllis Logan, Elaine's mother. Without whom we might have had no Elaine and no little Jennifer to toast."

Elaine explained briefly for Dirk's benefit what she had told the Serrills. "I couldn't help being disappointed about the way Phyllis and Carlos parted. They were so suited to each other that it seems a terrible pity that they broke up. It makes me feel that perhaps she didn't love him so much after all."

"I think she did," Paul said. "I think she showed a great deal of sense and maturity. Evidently they were very happy together, but happiness needs a context; it doesn't exist by itself or for itself. It grows from other things, interest in our work, our family and friends, concern for the society we live in. It's not an escape; it's a facing of life. I think Phyllis saw that the relationship between them had the effect of complicating lives for them and their families."

"But what an awful waste," exclaimed Elaine. "To undergo such an emotional strain and have nothing to show for it."

"It's not a waste when you learn something. Don't you think she drew strength and understanding from her love for Carlos that later enhanced her love for your father? I do. You know that sometimes a love can be a preparation for something else, for a deeper love to come. You don't necessarily stop loving that person, you don't *get over* love. But you can *add* to it. You learn from it; you grow through it, and if it is a good love you never lose it. It enriches the rest of your life, just as every experience does that you can learn from."

"That sounds so—so utilitarian," Elaine said.

"I agree with Paul," Doc said, pushing his chair back and lighting a pipe. " 'Build thee more stately mansions, oh my soul.' Why shouldn't another love be richer for the first?"

"Well, I'd better do the dishes," Elaine said, too embarrassed to pursue the subject in Dirk's presence. He had listened and said nothing but he watched her steadily, and she was suddenly acutely conscious of looking tired and bedraggled. She had gotten very little sleep in the last twenty-four hours and so much had happened since Frieda's outburst at the conference.

CHAPTER FOURTEEN

Back in her room, Elanie was weary but too restless to lie down. It was anxiety about Mrs. Hagstrom's verdict, she told herself, but she was also oppressed by her inability to understand Dirk. Ever since that telephone call after Matthew Crawford's illness she had been unable to comprehend Dirk's attitude toward her. She couldn't make up her mind whether his apparent indifference was real or whether he had simply decided it was no use campaigning against her stubbornness. And she admitted to herself that his indifference did not make her at all happy.

She had no idea how he spent his time outside of the office. As she thought of other girls, she realized how attractive he was, and pictured him pursued by various women and girls she had met or seen in town. That handsome red-haired proprietor of the book and record shop, the pretty librarian, the girl at Leo's who sang ballads, the young woman on the Board of Directors who had a roving eye—Elaine stopped summoning up these images in annoyance at herself. This was ridiculous.

She had clearly indicated to Dirk that she was not interested in him, regardless of her broken engagement, and she had meant it. But now she did care what Dirk thought of her; she wanted his approval . . .

To distract herself, she called Kitty to tell her about the baby and the delivery. Then it occurred to her that her father might read about the blizzard and be worried, so she put in a collect call to Chicago.

She could picture her father in his den overlooking Lake Michigan. He would have set aside his law journals and briefs by now to relax in his deep leather chair with his feet up on the hassock where she used to sit and talk with him in the evening. A cigar would be placed on the ashtray of his desk and beside it a plate with crackers, cheese, and a sliced apple.

"Hello!" The rasp of annoyance at the interruption changed to pleasure at the sound of his daughter's voice. "Elaine, I've just been reading about the storm there. Are you all right?"

"Oh, yes, Daddy. That's why I called, so you wouldn't be worried. And I've delivered a baby myself!" She talked on about the Serrills and Doc and how Dirk managed to bring Doc in spite of the blizzard.

"Who is this Dirk?"

Nonplused at her father's inquiry about Dirk, Elaine said quickly, "Oh, he's just a colleague of mine, sort of." She had intended to reserve the story of her mother's notebooks until she saw her father and could better judge how much or how little to disclose, but without meaning to she launched into an account of her discovery.

Her father was hardly an emotional type, but she had always been afraid of resurrecting his grief about her mother. Oddly enough, he accepted the news with an eager interest and a pleasure in talking about Phyllis that she would never have suspected. The idea was borne in upon her that time had healed the wound and now the memory of his wife was a comfort to him, as if he were finding her again in these new aspects —what might have hurt him years ago now was balm. Recognizing this, she said softly, "Daddy, I'll send you the notebooks and the album, and when I come home we'll go through them together." And then, "Oh, what a whopping telephone bill you'll have, Dad. I'll hang up now, but it was awfully good to talk to you again."

"That will be the most welcome bill I'll get," he said with gruff humor.

The next day Elaine tried to avoid thinking about Mrs. Hagstrom's verdict, but the question hung in her mind. When she came back in the afternoon Kitty gave her a wink.

"I saw Mrs. H. at the Welfare Office today, but I think she's back now."

Elaine took the hint and went down to the little office. In spite of her effort at composure, her heart was hammering and her smile uncertain. Mrs. Hagstrom had the three folders spread out on her desk. In her strictly professional mien that gentle face could look formidable, rigorous, and impassive.

"Good afternoon, Elaine. I notice here that your first recommendation to send Mrs. Hansom to a nursing home was later changed, or you recommended a delay. Was her health better or was there another reason for the shift?"

"I know it seems inconsistent," Elaine said apologetically, "but at first I didn't realize the ramifications of such a move. I didn't have any realistic idea about what effects it might have on the family and on Mrs. Hansom herself. When I learned more, it seemed to me that Mrs. Thompson might have had a breakdown . . . May I give you more details of the case?"

"If it is pertinent."

"Well, it seems that Mrs. Hansom disapproved of Hugh Thompson from the time the daughter met him years ago, and they defied her by eloping. They did well at first. Hugh was a good salesman and they bought a nice home in a good section, had Billy, and seemed quite happy. Mrs. Hansom was living alone in a New York apartment, and a few years ago she was diagnosed as a diabetic. Rosalind began to visit her occasionally and there was a reconciliation. One day Mrs. Hansom had a severe attack in her apartment and Rosalind went to take care of her."

Mrs. Hagstrom was following the records. "It was about this time that Hugh began drinking?"

"No, that came a little later. The illness kept Rosalind in New York for some time and Hugh reluctantly agreed to move the mother into his house until she was better. The grandmother never liked Billy and made no secret of it. This was when the boy began to have trouble at school. He played hooky, didn't do his lessons, began to look pale."

"But Mrs. Hansom has been there ever since."

"Yes, she gave up her apartment after another attack. Rosalind began to devote more and more time to caring for her mother, and it was about that time that Hugh began to go on binges. He lost his job but got another job within a short period. But it established a pattern. He would drink, lose his job, get another, drink more, find it harder to keep each job and harder to get a good one. The boy began to gain weight, but he seemed to settle down in school, and caused no more trouble."

"And I suppose the more Hugh was around home, the more bickering there would be."

"Yes, always about money and the boy and Mrs. Hansom. Hugh lost interest in the house he used to keep looking so nice, never mowed the lawn or painted or took care of repairs. Rosalind let the housekeeping go as she concentrated more on her mother, and their friends stopped coming around."

"Elaine, did you consult Frieda about this?"

"Yes, I did. I asked if she had any ideas about the case, and she thought it sounded as if Rosalind had a guilt complex about her mother, and was accepting the illness as a punishment for herself and her family for flouting Mrs. Hansom's

wishes. By this time, though Hugh was angry about the grandmother's attitude toward the boy, it was her money that half
supported them and she never let them forget it."

Mrs. Hagstrom tapped her pencil thoughtfully on the desk.
"Why didn't Frieda visit the home with you then?"

"That was the time she went home to visit her mother and
Dirk was coming with me as observer. Things he said made me
wonder if we didn't have to try to restore some morale in the
family before any attempt was made to move the mother to a
nursing home. Dirk thought that if Hugh's concern for the boy
was deep enough, he might assert himself and govern his drinking and regain some self-respect. Then maybe Rosalind would
revive her respect for him and stop her nagging and see things
in a different light, realizing that until her mother entered the
picture things had been going well with them. Dirk and I got
them both to see the psychiatrist at the Family Service Society
and there seemed to be some good results."

" 'Hugh has worked around the house, now has a good job,
drinks less,' " Mrs. Hagstrom read from the report. "What
about the boy?"

"Rosalind pays more attention to him now. She makes his
lunch and spends more time with him and he's begun to lose a
little weight. She's been stricter with her mother about medication too. I think Mrs. Hansom used her illness deliberately
to control the family, alarming them by refusing medication
and so on."

"It sounds extreme, but I think you're right."

Elaine's burden lightened a little at these words of agree-
ment and Mrs. Hagstrom went on: "I visited the family myself
and as far as I can judge, Frieda's charge was hysterical and
without any basis in fact. I believe Dirk's analysis was very
perceptive in this case. And I must say that I've been very impressed with the rough draft of his thesis, which I've read. He

presents some very persuasive evidence about other cases too." She pushed aside the folders. "You spoke of some changes in your ideas about nursing since you've come here, Elaine. Do you want to tell me more about that?"

"Yes, Mrs. Hagstrom, I'd like to." Although this was an unexpected invitation, Elaine had her father's adeptness in marshaling the elements of a case and his articulateness in presenting those elements. "I'm beginning to see that my experience has been valuable to me in a lot of ways. You see, I came here too unaware of the value of rapport with the patient, too blind to the need for working in the framework of the whole situation."

This was turning into a self-examination, but Elaine had the objectivity that made it possible for her to probe searchingly into her own character. "I have to admit it was a temperamental deficiency in me; I can't blame it on my limited hospital experience. My whole upbringing made me more self-centered and smug than any nurse—than any person—should be. I'd like to believe that this is behind me and that I've learned something. I honestly love the work, and my patients aren't just cases to me any more; I'm deeply concerned for them. I think I've learned more about myself and what kind of person I can become. If you feel I should resign, of course I would respect your judgment—but I want very much to continue here. *Very* much."

A smile restored the warmth to Mrs. Hagstrom's face, and after her ordeal Elaine could hardly believe what it signified.

"Elaine, it makes me very happy to hear you say that. Not everyone can see and admit mistakes and learn from them as wholeheartedly as you have. From the first I've been impressed with your grasp of our work, with your medical approach and your relations with the doctors; and it seemed to me that your success or failure in this field lay with your development of a more personal feeling for your patients and more understanding of their minds. I think now you are really on your way. Elaine, my dear, I feel as if today I am really welcoming you to the staff. And I want to congratulate you, too, on your handling of the delivery of the Serrill baby yesterday—Dr. O'Brien told me about it."

She walked to the door with Elaine, who could hardly have hoped for a better interview.

"Oh—Mrs. Hagstrom, what about Frieda? I hope this won't make things difficult for her."

"No, Elaine. I blame myself for not being more alert to her difficulties. I knew she was troubled about her mother, but I didn't realize that she hadn't been eating and sleeping properly or I would have insisted on a sick leave before she got herself into such a state. Being so exhausted, she took offense where none was meant, and she began to feel that she wasn't wanted or needed here. Of course she was mistaken, but she felt deeply hurt."

"Is there something I can do to help? I've learned a lot from her, and I'd like her to know that I appreciate it. I'm terribly sorry that all this happened, and I do feel responsibility for a large share of it, for I didn't let her know how much she'd done for me."

"Maybe you can find a way to tell her when she comes back. She'll be away for a week or two; I want her to get a good rest."

It appeared that the grapevine had reached upstairs, and her colleagues' genuine pleasure at the outcome was warming.

"What about Dirk?" someone said.

"I don't know but Mrs. Hagstrom was very complimentary bou his thes——"

"Exonerated too," came Dirk's voice from the door. "Elaine, ou left your folder on Mrs. H.'s desk." He laid it down on ers. From his manner she couldn't tell how she felt about her—

whether a truce still existed between them or whether he was interested in her only as a colleague. In any case she thought it only fair to let him know how glad she was that everything had worked out well.

As she said it, she knew that, under the layer of happiness about her interview with Mrs. Hagstrom, there was still another verdict that held her in suspense, and that was Dirk's.

"Cheers and all that for you too," he said in his most sardonic vein. "How about celebrating?"

There had been talk about a staff gathering that night at Leo's in celebration, but in some odd way Dirk's invitation took priority, which the others tacitly acknowledged. Elaine found Dirk helping her into her coat and escorting her out the door even while she was objecting that they could all celebrate together.

"Not tonight," he said decisively, and his manner intimidated her into meekness. When he steered her toward his old jalopy she didn't think of protesting that her V.N.A. car would be easier to handle in the slush and snow. Dirk closed the door and walked around to the driver's seat with a faint grin.

"Well, you *have* changed. You didn't turn a hair, did you? Can you stand the old-fashioned clutch and all that?"

"Oh, that." Pink crept over her face and she said primly, "The Chevrolet's low on gas anyhow." Now that she was alone with him, she wanted to be almost anywhere else. He was sure to lecture her about something—he always did.

Dirk headed the car out of town.

"Where are we going? Not to Leo's?"

"Later. There's something I want to show you. Maybe later we'll pick up Matt. He'll want to—celebrate too. "

The car turned up a road she had passed fifty times without notice, sandwiched as it was between heavy stands of pine near the reservoir. For once small talk didn't come easily to Elaine

186

but she didn't want Dirk to know how he affected her.

"Thank goodness it turned warm today. The sun must have melted half the snow by now. Oh, look at those crocuses over there peeping out of the snow. Wasn't it awful to have a storm just when spring was nearly here?"

A smile tugged at Dirk's mouth. "I don't know. I rather enjoyed it myself."

He turned off the road into a lane lined with tall elms and oaks, mounted a final little hill, swung around a curve, and stopped the car in a hollow between two rocky cliffs. Ahead of them was a rustic log house that caught the last rays of the sun. Twilight was settling in from the east.

"Who lives here? I don't think anyone's home, Dirk; there aren't any tracks."

Without answering he plunged through the snow and she followed him to the door. It was colder inside than out and the house was empty except for the furniture.

"An artist-friend of Matt's lived here and has just left for Italy. What do you think of the place?"

"I hardly know. It's different from everything else I've seen. Those cathedral windows are beautiful. And what a charming little balcony up there."

"Look around if you like."

From the paneled living room she went into the kitchen, compact but well equipped, glanced into a small bathroom, wandered into the dining room that was still receiving a little sunlight, and then went up the stairs. Off the balcony were two bedrooms and another bath. From the balcony she could see the tall pines and the lake.

"What a beautiful view from here, Dirk. What's beyond that door over there?" She pointed to the side of the room with the fireplace.

"Come and see." He opened the door into a double-height studio, which also overlooked the lake.

"What a lovely big room. How could that artist leave? Did he design all the furniture? I've never seen any like it." Without her realizing it, she had relaxed completely, happy to be with Dirk like this.

"Yes, and built some of it too. He's only leaving because he won a Prix de Rome. Do you like it?"

"It's so different . . . but, yes, I do like it. It seems to fit the house and setting so well, and the more I see it the better I like it. Like acquiring a taste for olives, you know—the sensation is so very unexpected and gradually you begin to like it for its very difference."

Footsteps sounded outside the door. Dirk crossed to open it, but he kept the man standing there while they spoke. Elaine politely averted her head and tried not to eavesdrop but a few words caught her ear—"check for deposit . . . call tomorrow . . . by the fifteenth . . ."

The man mumbled something in surprise, tipped his hat to Elaine when she turned, and went off while Dirk closed the door.

Goose pimples prickled on Elaine's arm, and without knowing why she felt herself growing tense, wanting to prattle senselessly and ward off some new, unknown event.

"That's settled," Dirk said, putting his wallet back into his pocket. "I think it's a good buy—five acres, a view, a six-room house with a terrace and a garage. I told the agent April fifteenth. That should be time enough, shouldn't it?"

"Time enough for what? What's this about April fifteenth. You mean you came here to buy this house?" She was bewildered, unprepared for the new situation that was building up. Dirk was always confronting her with some decision or other. "Would you mind explaining what you're talking about?"

"The house is for us. I thought of it when I met the artist last fall, and I've been wanting to show it to you but the time never seemed quite ripe—or maybe you weren't. I couldn't talk about it when you had just split up with Bryce. Or when you'd had that blow at Christmas about your patient. And later you were so busy with those epidemics—what could I do?"

Abruptly Elaine sat down; she wasn't sure her knees would support her anyhow. A wave of happiness flowed through her, before indignation made her sputter: "You mean you've been planning this all along and taking it for granted that I would marry you even after I told you— Oh, you make me so mad!" The gap between her uncertainty about his feeling for her and this disclosure was too much to cross in one leap, and unreasonably she grew angrier with every word he said.

Still grinning as if he thoroughly enjoyed her temper, he calmly continued, "Did I tell you I'm taking a job next fall with the County Health Department? Well, I figured you'd need a week or so to get used to the idea of marrying me. You'd want to tell your father and do some shopping—it won't be much of a ceremony on such short notice, but the minister has a Saturday afternoon free in ten days—and we can take a week's honeymoon and be back by the fifteenth to move in."

"Well, I think it's a lot of nonsense and you can get your check back and forget all about it." Elaine jumped up and started for the door, but he ambled along with her and quite casually set his foot against the door so that it wouldn't open to her tugging, which made her furious.

"You want more ritual? All right, Elaine, may I have your hand in marriage? Elaine, my lily maid—beg pardon"—his grin enraged her still more—"I mean my tiger-lily maid—now give me your answer and make it yes. Otherwise it will be a long time till dinner."

Elaine glared up at him, still not wanting to admit to him how she felt. "Oh, you are . . ."

"Watch your tongue, my sweet, you're speaking to your future husband." Then the mockery faded from his voice and eyes and he said quietly, "If you knew how often I've stood near you at the office like this, wanting to take you into my arms and kiss you—I can hardly believe there's nothing to interfere now. Except that temper of yours, and I'll take a chance on that."

She could remember the times. There had been a current between them then that was stronger than ever now, and she had a wild sensation of being drawn back into that whirlpool of emotion. She knew that she would yield this time, but she braced herself against the wall for one last stand: "How can you be so sure of yourself, so— What makes you think that I . . ."

"Chemistry and common sense." His voice was gentle but his arms were firm. "I knew I couldn't feel like this if there weren't some response from you, whether you admitted it or not. Remember your reaction to Phyllis and Carlos? And what Paul said about a love that is a preparation for another, about not getting over love but adding to it?" He kissed her ear. "There are many ways of saying yes, you know," he murmured and kissed her cheek and then her lips.

Elaine reached up and put her arms around his neck and kissed him back. All the uncertainty was gone; all of the rebellion melted within her; without daring all these months to admit it to herself, this was what she wanted above anything— Dirk's love.

COMPLETE LIST OF

ROMANCES FOR

YOUNG MODERNS

ALLISON DAY, WEATHER GIRL
> By NELL M. DEAN

AUTHORS' AGENT (Literary Agent)
> By ROBIN McKOWN

BALLET TEACHER
> By LEE WYNDHAM

BETTY LORING, ILLUSTRATOR
> By JESSICA LYON

A BUSINESS IN PETS (Running a Pet Shop)
> By NELL M. DEAN

A CAP FOR CORRINE (Registered Nurse)
> By ZILLAH K. MACDONALD

CONNIE, THEATRE DIRECTOR
> By KAREN VAN LISSEL

DANCE TO MY MEASURE (Choreographer)
> By LEE WYNDHAM

DATELINE: PARIS (Foreign Correspondent)
> By ALICE ROGERS HAGER

A FLAIR FOR PEOPLE (Personnel)
> By HELEN WELLS

GAY ENTERPRISES (Cooking and Baking)
> By MARJORIE MUELLER FREER

THE GIRL IN THE WHITE COAT (Medical Technologist)
> By HELEN WELLS

GLORIA, BALLET DANCER
> By GLADYS MALVERN

HOLLYWOOD STAR (Ballet)
> By GLADYS MALVERN

HOUSE OF HOLLY (Mail Order)
> By MARJORIE MUELLER FREER

INTRODUCING PATTI LEWIS, HOME ECONOMIST
> By HELEN WELLS

JANICE, AIRLINE HOSTESS
> By ALICE ROGERS HAGER

JOAN, FREE LANCE WRITER
> By ALICE ROSS COLVER

KAREN'S NURSERY SCHOOL PROJECT
> By BETTY K. HARRIS

KATHIE, THE NEW TEACHER
> By LUCILE G. ROSENHEIM

KATIE AND HER CAMERA (Photographer)
> By LOIS HOBART

KIT CORELLI, TV STYLIST
> By ELEANOR ARNETT NASH

LADY ARCHITECT
              By Lee Wyndham
LARK, RADIO SINGER
              By Helen Diehl Olds
LAURIE, PHYSICAL THERAPIST
              By Lois Hobart
LEE DEVINS, COPYWRITER
              By Mary Mannix
LINDA JORDAN, LAWYER
              By Jean Libman Block
LUCKY MISS SPAULDING (Fashion Retailing)
              By Eleanor Arnett Nash
MAGIC IN HER VOICE (Telephone Ad-Taker)
              By Pauline Panzer
MARCIA, PRIVATE SECRETARY
              By Zillah K. Macdonald
MARY ALLEN, PUBLICITY GIRL
              By Marcia Paul
"MISS LIBRARY LADY"
              By Ann McLelland Pfaender
NANCY RUNS THE BOOKMOBILE (Bookmobile Librarian)
              By Enid Johnson
NO PATTERN FOR LOVE (Fashion Designer)
              By Beryl Williams
ORCHIDS FOR APRIL (Horticulture)
              By Marjorie Mueller Freer
A PALETTE FOR INGRID (Fine Arts)
              By Lois Hobart
PRIMA BALLERINA
              By Gladys Malvern
THE RIGHT JOB FOR JUDITH (Settlement House Worker)
              By Enid Johnson
ROBERTA, INTERIOR DECORATOR
              By Marjorie Mueller Freer
ROSEMARY WINS HER CAP (Student Nurse)
              By Zillah K. Macdonald
ROXANNE, INDUSTRIAL NURSE
              By Zillah K. Macdonald
SALLY'S REAL ESTATE VENTURE
              By Enid and Margaret Johnson
SHOWCASE FOR DIANE (Display Artist)
              By Marjorie Mueller Freer
SUNNY, THE NEW CAMP COUNSELOR
              By Lucile G. Rosenheim
TOURS BY TERRY (Travel Agent)
              By Marjorie Mueller Freer
WASHINGTON SECRETARY
              By Alice Rogers Hager
WELCOME TO DUNECREST (Hotel Management)
              By Frances Leigh Williams
YOU CAN'T TELL ABOUT LOVE (Cosmetician)
              By Helen Diehl Olds

F ✓

DATE DUE		973 2212
7-23-71	12/23/75	2/28/85
11-15-72	5-3-77	3/28/85
4/3/73	12-2-80	10/16/86
11/27/73	12-8-80	
1/4/74	1-31-13	
3/5/74	12-10-83	
9-30-74	3-23-83	
10-7-74	4-14-83	
10-22-74	5-2-83	
1/27/75	11-8-83	
3/2/75	12-15-83	
12-7-76	4/4/84	

HOBART, LOIS

Elaine Forrest Visiting
Nurse